Entangled with a Texan

SARA ORWIG

Published by Silhouette Books
America's Publisher of Contemporary Romance

Laura Wright, Kathie DeNosky, Cindy Gerard, Cathleen Galitz and Kristi Gold— it was fun to work with you. Also, thanks to Liz Schultz and special thanks to my editor, Stephanie Maurer.

Special thanks and acknowledgment are given to Sara Orwig for her contribution to the TEXAS CATTLEMAN'S CLUB series.

SILHOUETTE BOOKS

ISBN 0-373-76547-9

ENTANGLED WITH A TEXAN

Copyright © 2003 by Harlequin Books S.A.

Visit Silhouette at www.eHarlequin.com

Printed in U.S.A.

This month, in
ENTANGLED WITH A TEXAN
by Sara Orwig

Meet David Sorrenson—
ex-military and notorious ladies' man. He'd hired
Marissa Wilder to help him watch over the little girl
left in his care. But having the sexy nanny living
under the same roof was tying this confirmed
bachelor in serious knots!

**SILHOUETTE DESIRE
IS PROUD TO PRESENT THE**

**Six wealthy Texas bachelors—all members of the
state's most exclusive club—must unravel the
mystery surrounding one tiny baby…and
discover true love in the process!**

* * *

**And don't miss
LOCKED UP WITH A LAWMAN
by Laura Wright
The second installment of the
Texas Cattleman's Club: The Stolen Baby series,**

available next month in Silhouette Desire!

Dear Reader,

Thank you for choosing Silhouette Desire—where passion is guaranteed in every read. Things sure are heating up with our continuing series DYNASTIES: THE BARONES. Eileen Wilks's *With Private Eyes* is a powerful romance that helps set the stage for the daring conclusion next month. And if it's more continuing stories that you want—we have them. TEXAS CATTLEMAN'S CLUB: THE STOLEN BABY launches this month with Sara Orwig's *Entangled with a Texan.*

The wonderful Peggy Moreland is on hand to dish up her share of Texas humor and heat with *Baby, You're Mine,* the next installment of her TANNERS OF TEXAS series. Be sure to catch Peggy's Silhouette Single Title, *Tanner's Millions,* on sale January 2004. Award-winning author Jennifer Greene marks her much-anticipated return to Silhouette Desire with *Wild in the Field,* the first book in her series THE SCENT OF LAVENDER.

Also for your enjoyment this month, we offer Katherine Garbera's second book in the KING OF HEARTS series. *Cinderella's Christmas Affair* is a fabulous "it could happen to you" plot guaranteed to leave her fans extremely satisfied. And rounding out our selection of delectable stories is *Awakening Beauty* by Amy J. Fetzer, a steamy, sensational tale.

More passion to you!

Melissa Jeglinski

Melissa Jeglinski
Senior Editor, Silhouette Desire

Please address questions and book requests to:
Silhouette Reader Service
U.S.: 3010 Walden Ave., P.O. Box 1325, Buffalo, NY 14269
Canadian: P.O. Box 609, Fort Erie, Ont. L2A 5X3

SARA ORWIG

lives in Oklahoma. She has a patient husband who will take her on research trips anywhere from big cities to old forts. She is an avid collector of Western history books. With a master's degree in English, Sara writes historical romance, mainstream fiction and contemporary romance. Books are beloved treasures that take Sara to magical worlds, and she loves both reading and writing them.

"What's Happening in Royal?"

NEWS FLASH, November—Strange things are afoot in Royal this month! Seems a woman collapsed the other night at our very own Royal Diner. Rumors are circulating that she had a baby and quite a load of cash on her. Who is she? Just what kind of trouble is this mysterious woman in? Unfortunately, our Jane Doe has not yet regained consciousness and the citizens of Royal can only speculate on the answers....

And what's going on at Royal's Texas Cattleman's Club? Some of our sexy gents were on hand to help Royal's Jane Doe and continue to keep a close eye on her. This reporter has tried to get a statement from recently returned member David Sorrenson, but he refused to comment on the proceedings except to say the Club was handling things....

Is David on baby-sitting detail? Reliable sources have spotted the notorious playboy shopping for baby clothes with an infant in tow. It's a good thing David has hired Marissa Wilder as the little girl's nanny. Marissa knows a thing or two about babies and is more than happy to help him out. Of course, what single gal in this town wouldn't jump at the chance to live under the same roof as this drool-worthy bachelor? Could this arrangement lead to something a bit steamier? Only time will tell....

One

Intuition told him that something was wrong. The last time he had felt this way was ten minutes before he had been pinned down by a sniper in a land far from home.

In spite of the good food and the great company, David Sorrenson shifted on his seat with an uncustomary restlessness. On more than one occasion, such hunches had saved his life, and he didn't like the hunch he was getting now. He tried to shrug it off as ridiculous. He was home safe and told himself to stop worrying.

The cold night on the third of November made the weekly chilifest at the Royal Diner even more appetizing. While vintage rock and roll played on the jukebox, the enticing smell of Manny's frying burgers permeated the local greasy spoon. Only a few booths were filled, and none of the red vinyl stools at the counter held customers.

In such a relaxed atmosphere, David couldn't explain the nagging uneasiness he was experiencing. It was good to be in his hometown of Royal, Texas, to be through with Special Ops, out of the air force and back with old friends.

David laughed at a joke Alex Kent was telling. His friend's green eyes sparkled. David had known Alex since they were kids. They were both thirty-five now, and their lives held a lot of similarities—no mother growing up, going all the way through school together, David involved with Special Ops and Alex, the FBI. Then, there were big differences. Alex, who drew the ladies like a flower draws bees, appeared completely comfortable with his life, while David didn't know why lately he had felt as if he were at a crossroads in his.

"David, you look like you're out in the south forty," Clint Andover said, curiosity in his blue eyes.

"Nope, I'm right here, but I was in the south forty all day hunting steers and it's good to sit and eat Manny's chili and listen to you two."

"Too bad Ryan couldn't join us," Alex remarked, referring to another of their friends.

"He's got a hot date tonight," David answered dryly, shifting his jeans-clad legs beneath the table. "He's going to rival you with the ladies, Alex."

The tiny brass bell over the front door tinkled, and David glanced that way. The door swung wide, causing a stir of the muslin curtains at the windows and allowing a blast of cold air to sweep into the restaurant. A woman clutching a baby and a diaper bag staggered into the diner.

"Oh-oh," David muttered, already sliding out of the booth, bracing himself on his booted feet, aware in his peripheral vision that his friends were up and moving as well.

Beneath a tangled mass of long, dark brown hair, the woman's head was bleeding—she looked as if she had fallen out of a car. Over a wrinkled blue-denim jumper, her bedraggled gray cloth coat was mud-spattered and torn. She was as pale as snow and looked on the verge of collapse.

Even as they rushed to her side, she began to fall. All three men reached for her.

Clint Andover caught her in his arms, and David grabbed

the tiny blanket-wrapped infant. Alex took the bulging diaper bag and already was on his cell phone calling for an ambulance.

When they caught her and the baby, the woman's eyelids fluttered. Large, thickly lashed violet eyes gazed up at them, and the only reason David heard her was because he was bending close as she whispered, "Don't let them take…my baby…don't let them get Autumn…."

Her eyelids fluttered again and closed as she went limp in Clint's arms.

Swaddled in a blood-spattered, torn pink blanket, the baby began to cry. While David gently patted the infant, Clint lowered the woman to the floor. Manny charged up with a grease-spattered topcoat.

"Here's a coat—"

While Clint took it to cover her, David continued patting the baby. To his surprise, the infant stopped crying, gazing up at him with wide, dark blue eyes.

"An ambulance is on its way," Alex said, and Manny moved away. Giving them plenty of room, diners stared in frozen shock while the three men tried to take care of the woman and baby.

Alex leaned down to the woman and took something crumpled from her fingers. David watched Alex straighten out the card. Startled, David met Alex's solemn gaze. When both men looked at Clint, a silent communication passed among them. David knew the other two also recognized the Texas Cattleman's Club card that the stranger had clutched in her hand.

As a member of the prestigious social club, David knew, as well as his friends, that the Texas Cattleman's Club was a facade. Its members worked together covertly on secret missions to save innocent lives. Tonight, two more close friends would have been with them, except Travis Whelan and Sheikh Darin ibn Shakir were out of the country on a confidential task. The woman lying on the floor of the Royal Diner was evidently here because she was seeking a Texas Cattleman's Club member to help her.

She had a dark bruise on one cheek, and Clint had his handkerchief pressed against the wound on her head. In the distance a siren wailed.

All of the diners still stood back so David didn't feel anyone could hear them if they talked softly. "She's here for help from the club," he said. "We can't just leave her."

"I agree," Clint replied, and Alex nodded.

"We have to ride in that ambulance with her. And we can't let them take the baby away from her," David continued.

"I've glanced in this bag she was carrying," Alex added quietly, with a grim note in his voice. "It has diapers and bottles and a little formula, but it's also stuffed with money. A damn lot of big bills."

David mumbled an expletive and tucked the baby into the crook of one arm. He hunkered down to take the woman's wrist and feel her pulse. When he looked at her pupils, he saw one was dilated more than the other.

"She's in bad shape," David said, looking at Clint and Alex. "Her pulse is weak."

"If something happens to her, we can't let the state take the baby until we know who gave her that card," Alex said.

"Call Justin Webb," David suggested, thinking of a fellow club member physician. "Tell him to meet us at the hospital and let's get him to check the baby. Even though babies aren't his usual patients—as influential as he is at Royal Memorial, he can step in and help us."

While Alex punched numbers, David said to Clint, "Take the baby." With his pararescue training, David didn't want to wait for the paramedics if the woman needed help. Before he could hand the infant to his friend, the bell over the door tinkled and two paramedics swept into the room. David recognized one of the medics and stood to speak to Carsten Kramer.

"Did anyone see what happened?" Carsten asked as the other paramedic knelt over the woman. David filled him in quickly while Clint put away his phone and nodded at David, indicating, to David's relief, that Justin Webb would meet them at the hospital. David watched while the medic checked the woman's airway, her pupils and her pulse.

Soon the paramedics had her hooked to an IV, and had an oxygen mask in place. They carefully put her on a transport board with a neck stabilizer and Clint Andover got permission to ride in the ambulance while David and Alex planned to follow in their cars. David passed the baby to a paramedic, feeling a peculiar reluctance to give up the infant even for a short time.

"Manny, we'll get the bill later," David called over his shoulder as he and Alex grabbed their jackets and rushed out behind Clint and the medics. Manny waved them away, following them outside and standing in his shirtsleeves, a spattered apron tied around his waist while he watched them.

Bright streetlights pushed back shadows and a sliver of moon hung in an inky sky above David's car, which was speeding toward Royal Memorial Hospital. The ride seemed interminable, yet David knew the hospital was located within walking distance of the Royal Diner. Where had the woman come from? Who had given her the card? Questions plagued him during his dash toward the emergency entrance.

Carrying the diaper bag, Alex jogged to join him and together they rushed into the hospital just as the paramedics were wheeling the unconscious woman down the hallway through double doors. David and Alex met Clint and were told they would have to wait.

In less than three minutes, a familiar tall, brown-haired man, Justin Webb, M.D., came striding through the door and shook hands with all three men.

"Thanks for coming so quickly," David said. "They've already taken the woman and baby to an examining room."

"Who is she?" Justin asked.

David quickly filled Justin in on what had happened at the diner.

"Sounds like what started out as a peaceful night in Royal has turned out to be a big problem dumped on you guys,"

Justin said quietly. He nodded at David. "Okay, I'll see about the baby."

"Thanks!" David exclaimed with relief. "Just let us take care of the baby until the mother can."

Justin frowned. "If the mother can't keep the infant for a few days, I'll see to it that y'all can," he stated, his solemn gaze sweeping the other three Texas Cattleman's Club men before he turned to stride away.

"He'll keep that promise if humanly possible," David said, staring after the tall doctor who was one of the Southwest's leading plastic surgeons and responsible for Royal Memorial's Plastic Surgery/Burn Unit.

"He's been through this with his own," Alex added as the three men headed for chairs to sit and wait.

David knew that the others were as aware as he that Justin's oldest child, Angel, now adopted, was left on his wife's doorstep before Justin and Winona were married.

"Justin and Winona adore that little girl of theirs," Clint said.

"I think Justin will do everything in his power to see to it that this baby doesn't have to go to the Child Protective Services," David added.

As the three men waited, Alex Kent pulled out his cell phone. "Even though we need to keep a low profile on this as much as possible, it's only a matter of time until the police are notified. I'm surprised they're not here now. I'll call Wayne Vicente and talk to him because we've worked together before."

"Good idea, Alex," Clint said.

David leaned back and crossed his long legs, listening to his friend talk to the police chief. Even though they were the only people in the waiting room, Alex spoke in a low voice. David glanced at his friends. They were in jeans, Western shirts and boots just as he was—standard dress for chili night at the diner.

As soon as he finished the call, Alex put away his phone. "Vicente will be here shortly."

"I've been thinking about the woman," Clint said. "If they hold her here at the hospital—or if she's unable to leave—with all that money and a head wound and the card, she must be in danger. When they put her in a room, I think one of us should guard her."

"That's good," David said. "What about it, Clint? You're our security guy, anyway."

Clint shrugged. "I can arrange my schedule so I can stay. Sure. I'll do it."

"Okay," Alex said, shifting the diaper bag underneath his chair. "I'll deal with the police and put the money in a safe place unless Vicente takes it. Or until the mother can manage on her own."

"I can help you," David volunteered.

"David, you take care of the baby," Clint said. "One of us has to." ·

"If it comes to that," David answered, expecting the baby to be put in the room with the mother before the night was over.

The three friends fell silent, each lost in his own thoughts until Alex stood and crossed the room to the door. A uniformed man entered the waiting room, and David watched as Alex greeted the stocky, brown-haired police chief.

Talking briefly, the two men crossed the room. David stood to greet the chief.

"You remember David Sorrenson and Clint Andover," Alex said.

"Sure do. Talked to you, Clint, what—was it just three or four days ago?" Chief Vicente said as he extended his hand.

"Something like that," Clint answered, shaking the police chief's thick hand.

"Here's the bag with the money," Alex said, and all four sat down while Vicente unzipped a turquoise-and-pink diaper bag. The police chief whistled. "The lady must be in a heck of a lot of trouble. This is a fortune."

"We don't know anything about her, but we want to help

her," Clint replied solemnly. "There must have been a reason for her to come to Royal."

Chief Vicente rubbed his forehead. "Okay, Alex. I'll file a report and let you know if I have to do anything else. If not, go ahead and put the money in a safe place and keep me posted on what's happening. I'll talk to the doc now and see about the woman and baby."

"Thanks," Alex said.

All three men stood, offered thanks, and then sat down as the chief left and headed through the door marked for hospital staff only.

It was another half hour before a nurse appeared, crossing the room to face the men. "Dr. Webb sent me to get you. Are you the men he wants to see?"

"We are," Clint replied as they stood and followed her down a brightly lit hall into an examining room. She closed the door behind them and they were alone with Justin and the baby. Holding her, Justin was giving the baby a bottle.

"This little girl is healthy and hungry," he said. "I'm glad you called me. This baby can't be more than five to ten days old, because the umbilical cord hasn't dried up yet. The mother is in a coma so she can't care for her baby right now."

With a sinking feeling in the pit of his stomach over Justin's gloomy news, David looked at the tiny baby, knowing he wasn't the one to take charge of a baby. He tried to focus on Justin as the doctor continued talking.

"The doctors don't have any identification. They don't know how she got into town or where she came from. She wasn't carrying a purse?" Justin looked at them questioningly.

David shook his head. "We don't know any more than you do, Justin."

"When they move her, I'm going to stay and guard her room tonight," Clint said. "We think she's in danger. And it looks like this is going to take longer than we thought. We expected her to clear up all the questions within the next few hours."

"I don't think so," Justin replied. "They'll put her in ICU, the Intensive Care Unit, but it's still a good idea to stand guard. If someone was intent on harm, he could get to her. Her condition is listed as critical."

"Oh, hell," David exclaimed, remembering the desperate look in her violet eyes.

"Her doctor, Harry McDougal, thinks she suffered the blow to the head by a blunt instrument, so you're probably right that she's on the run, trying to get away from someone," Justin continued.

"She called the baby Autumn," Clint said, and all four men looked at the baby.

"Ah, little Autumn," Justin said, smiling at the little girl in his arms. "Okay, guys. Clint's staying at the hospital to guard our mystery woman."

"I'm taking care of the money, and I'll use my resources to find out what I can about her," Alex explained.

"Okay," Justin said. "So who gets little Autumn?"

"I guess I'm the guy, but I don't know one thing about babies," David admitted. "Any of you want to trade jobs?" he asked, a desperate feeling growing inside of him.

"We've got our assignments," Alex answered, looking amused. "C'mon, David, it's time you have some shaking up in that orderly life of yours."

"Yeah, orderly," David remarked, staring at the baby. "Last year I was getting shot at and feeling thankful just to be alive."

"It's quiet here in Royal," Alex said. "You get the baby. Besides, neither one of us is a baby expert. Nope, we've got our assignments, and we'll leave you with Justin now so you can get your instructions."

"Hey! You two, wait a minute," David exclaimed, feeling a momentary panic as his friends walked toward the door. "No kidding. I've never even held a baby."

"Then it's time you did," Alex said. "We'll head out to do our jobs and leave you to yours. We better plan a meeting, though."

"Right. Tomorrow morning," David replied darkly, staring

at the bundle in Justin's arms. All he could see was a small round head with wisps of light brown hair showing. "You guys meet me at the club at noon tomorrow."

"We'll be there," Clint promised as the two walked away. "Thanks, Justin."

"Yeah, thanks, man," Alex added, and closed the door behind them.

"I don't know what to do with a baby," David repeated, his hands on his hips. "I'm trained for the stuff those guys are doing."

"Just feed and change her and hold her and you'll do fine," Justin said.

"When do I feed her? Breakfast, lunch and dinner?"

"Where've you been living—under a rock? Don't any of those gorgeous women you date have babies around?"

"No, they don't. And there were none in my family," David added tersely, wondering if there was any way to get out of keeping her.

"I imagine this little girl is going to want a bottle every couple of hours."

"Every two hours!" David exclaimed, astonished and appalled and wondering how he was going to cope.

Justin looked as if he was struggling to keep a straight face. "Yes, David. Now, let me show you how to change a diaper and the umbilical cord dressing," Justin said, turning to carefully place the baby on the examining table while David moved close beside him.

After fifteen minutes, Justin let go a guffaw. "Damnation, man! It's simple. I'll bet that even blindfolded you could put that rifle you carried, night scope and all, together in seconds and take it apart again, so I know you've got the dexterity and brains to catch on how to put these little diapers on this tiny little person."

"A rifle is a hell of a lot simpler," David snapped. "And she keeps kicking her legs all the time. A rifle just lies there."

"You'll get it. You made it through U.S. Air Force Special Ops training so I know you'll get this. I seem to remember a degree from Harvard, too. So come on, pull your wits together and try again. And by the way, she's being very good-natured about this. By now, most babies would be complaining loudly enough to be heard on the next floor. You've got a little doll here," Justin added, his voice changing to a gentler note. "I miss having a baby."

"Well, why don't—"

"No way. Don't even suggest it," Justin said firmly, shaking his head. "Winona would throw me out the door. I can't go home with a baby that we know we'd have to give up soon. Now, you change that diaper. Put all your Special Ops skills and your years of education into this."

"I'm beginning to be sorry I called you. Nothing at Hurlburt Field or anywhere else prepared me for this. Look how tiny she is. I'm scared I'll hurt her."

"No, you won't. She isn't going to break," Justin replied with a grin. "Just be careful—like you were with your M16 or whatever lethal weapon you carried. David, I read somewhere that the Air Force Special Ops training dropout rate is almost eighty percent. That means only a little more than twenty percent make it. You're one who did. Now, if you can do that, you can do this."

"A baby is entirely different," David said grimly through clenched teeth. "She won't stay still." He struggled with the diaper, finally getting it in place and watching, letting out his breath when it didn't spring loose. "There!"

"Congratulations! You got it! I knew you could do it!" Justin exclaimed, slapping David lightly on the back.

"Can it, Webb," David snarled, frowning. "Now, what else do I need to know?"

"Do you know how to mix her formula?"

"Her what?"

"Why does your question surprise me?" Shaking his head, Justin picked up a six-pack of cans. "Here's formula. I'll send you home with a goodly supply. The directions for mixing it are on the can. I'll give you a supply of diapers and bottles—

the hospital has plenty to send home with new mothers. And I guess you're as new a mother as anyone could be.''

''She can't just drink milk from the fridge?'' David asked, holding up a can of formula and reading the instructions.

''No, she can't drink milk from the fridge,'' Justin replied patiently. ''And there are other things. Tomorrow, you're going to need to get the little girl some clothes, unless there are some things buried in the bag with all that money Alex was talking about.''

''Great balls of fire! How could a little tiny person require so much stuff and so much attention?'' David exclaimed, shocked by all that was going to be required and wondering what he had gotten himself into.

''My friend, if you have her more than three days, you're never going to want to tell her goodbye.''

''I don't think so,'' David said, eyeing the baby, whose eyes had closed. ''Is she all right?''

''She's asleep. I've fed her, and you wore her out with your diaper practice. Now, let's pack you up and let me get home to my own family.''

''Justin, thanks for this. And can I call you if I have questions?''

''Yes, but just relax. She's a sweetheart.'' Justin slanted him a quizzical look. ''You don't have a baby carrier, do you?''

''A what?''

''I don't know why I even asked. You can't just set her in the car seat beside you. You need something to hold her safely. I'll bet I can find a nurse with one that you can borrow. Just stay put until I get back.'' David was handed the sleeping infant. He took her, cradling her with his arm and marveling at how tiny she was.

''How can she possibly be so complicated when she's small enough to hold in my hands?'' David asked, but his friend had already gone through the door. David stared at the infant.

''I'll do my best, and I'm sorry you've got someone who doesn't know one thing about a baby,'' he said softly. Her tiny hands were folded over her middle and David was awed by her. So tiny, yet so perfect and so pretty. He touched her cheek lightly with his finger. "So soft and sweet," he whispered.

In minutes Justin was back to give David final instructions. "Stop worrying," Justin said, smiling. "You'll get along fine."

"Right. See you, Justin." David went to find Alex and get whatever in the diaper bag belonged to the baby. And then he told his friends goodbye and left the hospital, stepping out into the chilly Texas night. He looked at the sleeping infant.

"What am I going to do with you?" he asked her softly.

He drove through the dark night, thankful she slept, but with his nerves on edge. He dreaded when she would wake because he had zero experience in baby care.

His sprawling ranch house had motion lights that came on as he approached the back of the property. At the back gate David parked and got out, taking baby, carrier and supplies with him. He crossed the wraparound porch and unlocked the back door, dropping supplies on a credenza in the back entryway while he turned off the alarm and switched on lights.

In minutes he was in his big bedroom with the baby carrier in the middle of his king-size bed.

Baby and carrier looked out of place, he reflected, in this masculine room with its hunter-green-and-brown decor. He scratched his head, wondering what to do when she wakened and began to cry. As he thought about it, the tiny girl stirred and in seconds was crying.

David unbuckled her and picked her up, changing her with a little more ease this time in spite of her crying and kicking.

He got her a bottle, fed her and placed her in his big bed, climbing in beside her. Exhausted, he fell asleep for what seemed like ten minutes and then the infant was crying again.

By three in the morning, the kitchen was a shambles of half-full bottles, cartons the bottles came in, baby clothes that she had spit up on. While she screamed and cried, he paced the floor, and in minutes warmed another bottle to try again to get her to quiet down.

"Oh, little baby, what do you want?" he asked wildly, knowing if he called Justin, he would just get laughed at.

At four he placed her in his bed again. She had fallen asleep and David eased down on the bed beside her, scared he would either wake her or roll over on her, but totally exhausted. Once more, he felt he'd only slept a few minutes, but it was an hour later that her cries woke him.

The night seemed three hundred hours long and by morning, David knew he had to find a nanny.

Through the sleepless night he had racked his brain for any woman he had dated whom he could call for help, but he couldn't come up with one likely candidate who would want to deal with a baby.

He turned in an ad to the paper for a nanny, knowing that it would take days before the ad would produce inquiries. His full-time cook and housekeeper arrived and tried to help, but at sixty, Gertie Jones was still single and knew almost as little about babies as David.

As soon as possible, he drove into Royal, heading to a local baby store to get supplies.

Since getting out of the military and returning home, David usually took pleasure in driving through his hometown of Royal, Texas. Main Street was a bustling place in the exclusively rich West Texas town, which was surrounded by oil fields and ranches. Today, under bright skies and sunshine, he passed the Royalty Public Library, a one-story, Georgian-style brick building in the center of town, and the Royalton Hotel on Main Street, a fancy old hotel that dated back to 1910, but he didn't see any of his surroundings. He was a man with a mission, as dead set on getting help as he had ever been on accomplishing any assignment in his life.

David waited in his car until the baby store unlocked and opened its doors, then he and other customers rushed inside. Feeling lost, he hurried down aisles past tiny dresses and small suits until he reached a section with diapers, little shirts and rattles. While he was searching for a clerk, Autumn began to cry.

"Oh, please don't cry," David said. Frantically, he hunted for a clerk, turning a corner and starting up another aisle, jiggling Autumn in his arms as she refused the bottle and continued crying.

"Little baby, don't cry!" David was desperate. He hadn't shaved this morning and was barely dressed; he'd thrown on whatever shirt he could grab and old jeans. He suspected his hair was sticking straight up in the air, but that was of small consequence at the moment.

"Aw, Autumn, baby, don't cry," he pleaded. He heard someone moving and saw a clerk bending down behind a counter. He rushed for her as if he were drowning at sea and had spotted a raft.

"Can you help me?" he asked, hoping he didn't sound too alarmed.

The clerk straightened, and David stared at her in shock while she gazed back wide-eyed at him.

Two

The woman was wearing a pink sunbonnet the likes of which he had seen only in movies or in pictures of his great-great-grandmother. She had on a flowered, frilly dress covered with lace and pink velvet bows. Her dark blond hair was tied in long pigtails with pink bows and each cheek had bright rose circles. Her lashes looked too thick for her to be able to open her eyes, black feathery lashes that framed lively chocolate-brown eyes that gazed at him with a curious intensity. She had a luscious, deep red rosebud mouth.

In turn, Marissa Wilder gaped at David Sorrenson, taking in all six feet two inches of the ruggedly handsome man. Her heart thumped faster, and her temperature rose. How old had she been when he'd first had this effect on her? She was probably eleven years old. At eighteen, he had barely known she was alive. As a matter of fact, she suspected that right now he didn't have a clue who she was. But was he a sight for female eyes! More handsome than ever with his thick, wavy raven hair and sexy sea-green eyes.

Then she became aware of the tiny baby in his arms. The little one was bawling at the top of its lungs and he simply stood there and looked helpless and desperate. Where was the man's wife? Coming out of her spell, Marissa reached out.

"Let me hold your baby," she said, taking the infant from his hands.

"Is there a microwave oven in this store where I can heat a bottle for her?" he asked. He fumbled in the brown paper sack he was carrying and fished out a bottle.

"Yes, there is," Marissa answered, taking the bottle and motioning to him to follow her. David trailed after her to a tiny lounge with chairs covered in yellow vinyl and signs to employees lining the walls. He watched her warm the bottle and then take it out of the microwave to give it to the baby.

She cuddled the baby in her arms and placed the bottle close, letting the nipple touch the baby's cheek. The little one turned her head the fraction needed, found the nipple and began to suck.

Quiet settled and Marissa gazed down at the baby. Longing filled her. How much she wanted her own baby! She yearned for a child. She forgot the man watching her as all her attention settled on the child. Yielding to her imagination, she wished the baby was her own precious darling.

"You're a natural with her," said a deep voice that yanked her out of her reverie, and she looked up into green eyes that now were fully focused on her. David Sorrenson looked as if he wanted to devour her, and her breath caught.

"A natural?"

"With babies," he said, nodding his head as he looked at the baby in her arms.

"Oh, well, I've been around a lot of them. I have one niece and three nephews and two younger sisters," Marissa answered. "She's a precious baby. Where's your wife?"

"I'm not married. And she's not my baby. Well, she is for now."

Marissa stared at him, realizing the man was distraught. This was rather shocking, because she had been to more than a few football games when he had been a senior and quarter-back of the Royal High team and he had always remained cool and unflappable. She had been much younger, but she had heard her older sisters talk about him and she had seen him play football. She studied him. He needed a shave. His shirt wasn't buttoned correctly. He ran his fingers through his tangled mop of black hair while he continued to stare at her as if she were a bug under a microscope.

"Are you married?" he blurted.

"No, I'm not," she answered, beginning to wonder if he was under some kind of mental pressure that was causing him distress. "I'm divorced."

Her answer seemed to relieve him, but she couldn't imagine why, because she knew all too well, he didn't want a date. He thrust out his hand.

"I'm David Sorrenson."

"Yes, I know," Marissa said, feeling her hand enveloped in his large, warm one. The contact was as disturbing to her jangled nerves as his steadfast gaze. "You were in school with one of my older sisters. I'm Marissa Wilder. You were in high school with Karen."

"You don't say. I didn't recognize you. You're a natural with babies, though. And you seem to like them."

"I love babies," she said softly, looking at the little girl in her arms. "What's her name?"

"Autumn," he replied.

"Autumn. That's a lovely name. How old is she?"

"Five to ten days probably, give or take a few."

Give or take a few? What kind of daddy was he? she wondered, some of her illusions about David Sorrenson shattering. "And you've been sent out to buy some diapers?" Marissa guessed.

"Something like that. Have you worked here long?"

"About two years," she said. If she didn't know whom she was talking to, she would summon the store security guard. David's questions were weird, and she clearly recollected a lot of female discussion through the years about David Sorrenson. Never once had the description "weird" been included.

"Would you like a job as a nanny?" he blurted. "I need one badly and I'll pay extremely well. Whatever you're making here, I'll triple it."

After moments of silence ticked past, Marissa realized she was staring at him with her mouth open. Dumbstruck by his offer, she was momentarily speechless. "Triple my salary?" she repeated finally.

"Yes. You seem to know how to deal with a baby and I don't. I need help."

If it had been anyone else on earth, Marissa would have sent him packing, but for the better part of seventeen years of her twenty-eight-year-old life, she had had a schoolgirl crush on David Sorrenson. Once again, she was speechless. Work for him? Triple her salary?

"This is sort of sudden. Do you mean to come to your house every day?"

"No. I mean to live in my house and care for Autumn daily."

"Oh!" *Live* in David Sorrenson's house? "Be still my beating heart," she whispered.

"What's that?" he asked sharply, studying her even more closely.

Her brain began to function again. "I'm sorry, but I can't do that. My folks are out of the country, and I take care of my grandmother and my younger sisters."

"Maybe they can all move to my house. How old are your sisters?"

"My grandmother won't move," she replied, thinking he had the most sinfully seductive eyes she had ever seen. Cool, clear green with a thick fringe of long, black lashes. "Greta is a junior in college, and Dallas is a senior in high school."

"The junior in college is old enough to take care of your grandma and your youngest sister."

"Well, that's true," Marissa reasoned. "When do you want someone to go to work for you?"

"This morning."

Again she stared at him. The man's mind must have slipped a cog in the past few years. Although, physically, he still looked extremely well put together. Those were very broad shoulders. "I have a job. I can't walk out on the store."

"I'll pay you to walk out. I'll talk to the manager and straighten it out with him," David said decisively. "I'll give you an extra thousand-dollar bonus to leave your job this morning."

"A thousand dollars? Just like that?" She stared at him, still stunned by his sudden offer and his snap decisions.

"Just like that. I'm desperate," he replied.

"I'm beginning to believe you are." Her head swam now. He had stepped into her world and turned it upside down. Triple her salary. Live with David Sorrenson. A thousand dollars. She had heard the man had retired from Air Force Special Operations. He was independently wealthy, living on his ranch. There were two or three women in town whom he had been seen with—wealthy, sophisticated beauties. Marissa hadn't heard any remarks about his mental condition. Or that he had a baby.

Triple her salary. A thousand dollars. Live in his house. The offer spun in her thoughts repeatedly. That last thing—live in his house—she knew she should avoid, because that was the road to heartbreak. As distraught as he was and as rumpled and unshaved and uncombed, he was still a hunk. But weird. On the other hand, enjoy the moment, she thought.

"I don't know about leaving my job right this minute," she replied cautiously, her mind racing over the possibilities. "This is a drastic decision. I think you and I need to sit down and discuss your offer."

"Okay. Tell the manager that you're taking a break and we'll go confer about the nanny job. It'll be very temporary, probably only a day or two at the most."

"A day? Then you don't really need a nanny."

"Oh, yes, I do!" he snapped. "I can't go through another

night like last night. Actually, I don't want to go another hour without help.''

The man was unhinged, but nonetheless, for the money he was offering, she was interested.

"We do need to discuss this," she said, leading him out of the employees' break room and going back to her station.

"We can go to the Royal Diner to talk. Have you had breakfast?"

"No, I didn't eat breakfast this morning," she replied, dazed by what was happening and barely thinking about breakfast.

"Want me to tell your manager?" David asked, looking around the store.

"Oh, no!" she gasped, imagining her supervisor's reaction to all this. "I'll tell him. You take Autumn."

"No," David replied in a no-nonsense, take-charge voice. "You hold Autumn and keep feeding her because she's happy. I'll tell the manager and square it with him and I'll drive. What's your manager's name?"

"Jerry Vickerson, and his office is in the southeast corner of the store."

"I'll be right back, Marissa Wilder. Don't go away," David ordered, giving her a look that immobilized her as he started to walk away. "And when I get back, I need to buy a baby carrier for her before I leave the store. I don't care about the price. You pick it out."

Turning to stride away, he combed his fingers through his hair and squared his shoulders.

"Baby Autumn, you have a very decisive, persuasive caretaker. Where's your mommy, sweetie?" A nanny with triple her current salary. Wow. It wasn't going to do her 401K any good, but to take care of this little baby would be wonderful. To live at David Sorrenson's would be—exciting? Heartbreaking, most likely. She probably would spend half her time fantasizing about him. Although, his behavior this morning hadn't made him too adorable. Still, the man had gotten what he wanted in no time flat.

As she cuddled the baby close against her, Marissa hummed to herself while she selected a carrier. She remembered the brown paper sack David had had in his hand and picked up a pretty pink diaper bag with teddy bears on it.

In minutes he came striding back. "It's settled. Your job is terminated. You can have it back whenever this nanny job ends—which may be soon."

She stared at him in amazement. Her boss was just a step away from being a modern-day Ebenezer Scrooge to his employees. To have him suddenly become so cooperative surprised her, and she wondered what incentive David Sorrenson had offered her boss.

"All right," she said cautiously. "I picked out this carrier and here's a diaper bag. You look as if you need one," she said, eyeing the paper sack.

"Oh, yeah, I do. Good." He pulled out his wallet and glanced at the price tags. "That's good. I'll transfer this stuff from the sack to the bag and then, when we get to my car, we'll put Autumn into the carrier. I'm using a borrowed one that I need to return."

Marissa rang up his purchase with one hand, completing the transaction and watching him empty the sack and toss it into the trash.

"Do you want to get your things and leave your name tag?" David asked. "I told your manager I would bring you back later to pick up your paycheck. He said he would have it ready in an hour."

She realized David was waiting and she hurried to get her purse. "You'll have to hold the baby for me. I need both hands free to get this name tag off."

"Let me do it," David said, stepping close.

Her pulse jumped as he moved within inches. His warm fingers brushed her collarbone and her shoulder. He stood close and she looked at his unshaven jaw covered in black stubble, his mouth with his slightly full lower lip, the sight of which stirred a bushel of curiosity about how those lips would feel on hers. He deftly removed the pin and placed it under the counter. "Anything else?" he asked.

"Oh, yes!" she answered dreamily while looking at curls of dark chest hair at the open neck of his blue, short-sleeved western shirt and thinking she could let his fingers flit over her for another half hour or so.

"Yes?" he repeated, his voice filled with curiosity while he stared at her with arched brows. Then she realized what she had just said.

"I meant no!" she replied swiftly, feeling her cheeks flush. She turned away, but not before she saw his eyes narrow and his gaze became more piercing than ever.

He took her arm. "My car is this way."

She had a ridiculous feeling she had just lost control of her life. All because she knew how to feed and hold a baby. "Don't you like babies?"

"I don't know anything about them. Well, now I know they cry a lot and I know how to change a diaper."

Marissa hurried beside him, trying to keep up with his long-legged stride as they left the store and crossed the parking lot to his low-slung, dark green sports car. Sunshine spilled over them on the crisp November day, and Marissa still couldn't believe what was happening to her. She glanced over her shoulder at the store and it seemed as if she were in a dream. Why wasn't she back there working?

She looked at the tall man beside her. In less than thirty minutes he had changed her life. Now here she was outside, invited to breakfast with an unbelievably appealing man and she was going to get to care for a precious little girl and make a lot of money doing it. She had to be dreaming, yet the sunshine was warm and very real. Enjoy the moment, she thought.

He held the door for her. "I'll take Autumn now and put her into her carrier." Once again, their hands touched and she was too aware of each tiny contact. What was happening to her? She didn't usually have that reaction when she handed things to men at the store.

She looked down at her clothes. Did she want to go to the

Royal Diner in her Bo-Peep costume she had worn for the store special today? Deciding she would, she sighed. It was her own outfit, not the store's, and it would be too complicated to go home to change.

Climbing into the car, Marissa watched David put the baby into her new carrier in the back seat. He buckled the infant and the carrier in and then slid behind the wheel.

Beware of charming, appealing men, she reminded herself silently, glancing at David. She remembered how she had fallen head over heels in love—or had it been infatuation?—for her handsome ex-husband who had turned out to be a crushing disappointment in her life. A man who had used her for his own purposes, cheating on her while she worked to help put him through medical school. When he'd achieved his goal, he had discarded her, hurting her badly.

When Autumn began to cry, Marissa twisted in the seat to talk to the baby and to try to give her the bottle. As soon as she did, Autumn became quiet.

"Thanks for doing this," David said.

"She's an adorable baby. So pretty."

He didn't answer, and in minutes they whipped into a parking place in front of the Royal Diner. "I'll take the carrier inside with us," he said, climbing out to unbuckle the carrier. While he held the door for Marissa, she entered the warm Royal Diner. With every step she was aware of David's presence, aware of brushing against his arm as she went through the open door.

When the smell of frying bacon and brewing coffee assailed her, she realized that she was hungry. Sliding into a booth, Marissa smoothed her skirt and petticoats and patted the seat. "Put Autumn's carrier here beside me. When she finishes this bottle, I can watch her."

He didn't need any arm-twisting for that one. Instantly, he set the carrier with the sleeping baby beside Marissa and then he slid into the booth and sat facing her.

Feeling nervous and self-conscious, Marissa smiled at him.

She glanced around the diner and saw a familiar waitress heading toward them.

Popping gum and giving a tug to her tight, pink polyester uniform, Sheila Foster brought them glasses of water and plastic-coated menus. "Hi, Marissa. Hi, David," she greeted them, looking again at Marissa. "Cute dress and cute baby."

"Thanks, Sheila," Marissa said with a big smile that revealed a dimple in her right cheek.

"Would you like coffee?" Sheila asked.

David nodded, still staring at Marissa's dimple. "What about you, Marissa?"

Every time he said her name in his deep voice, a tingle slithered through her middle. She shook her head. "No, thanks. I'll have a glass of orange juice."

"I'll have orange juice with my coffee," David added.

As soon as they were alone, Marissa asked him, "So, David, how are you related to Autumn?"

David met Marissa's gaze squarely. "I'm not," he answered carefully, realizing that for once in his life, he hadn't thought ahead to explanations.

"She's not related to you," Marissa repeated, and there was no mistaking the surprise in her voice. "So how come she's in your care?"

The woman might dress strangely, David thought, but her brain was clicking right along. And those dark brown eyes of hers were slicing into him. He weighed what to reveal and what to keep to himself.

"I was here last night with friends, and while we were eating, a woman came rushing in and collapsed."

"This is *her* baby?" Marissa demanded. "That was on last night's news. How did *you* get the baby? Why isn't she with her mother?"

He had been so distraught over feeding and caring for Autumn, he hadn't considered how fast the word would spread in Royal. Royal might be a town filled with some of the greatest wealth in the Lone Star State, but it was still a small place and news traveled like wildfire.

"I know Dr. Justin Webb," David answered carefully. "When my friends and I took the woman and her baby to the hospital, we met with Dr. Webb. Instead of turning the baby over to a state agency, he said I could take care of her until her mother is able to," he explained.

"Wow! No wonder you looked a little upset."

"Yeah, well, I haven't spent time around a baby before. I haven't ever even held one before last night."

Marissa looked at sleeping Autumn as if she was filled with sympathy for the little girl. "Well, I'm here now and I've held plenty of babies," she said, with a confident tone that was reassuring to him. "We better discuss this job I'm supposed to do. I guess you want me to move in today."

"Damn straight I do," he said with heartfelt sincerity. "I'll be counting the minutes."

"I have to go home, break the news to my family, pack, get my family arranged and then I'll be over. Maybe four today. How's that?"

"Fine, but if you get there sooner, it'll be great."

"You don't have a girlfriend who could do this?" she asked curiously.

"No, I don't. None of the women I date is into babies and diapers and formula. Not even remotely."

"I can imagine," she said, and again, David wondered what she thought of him. In her eyes he might be an irresponsible playboy. "The mother is all alone in a coma in the hospital?" Marissa asked.

"Not altogether alone. One of my friends, Clint Andover, is standing watch."

Marissa nodded in approval. "What are my hours?"

Startled, he stared at her. "All the time, I thought."

She shook her head. "I have a family and I want some time off."

He tilted his head to study her, desperation looming inside him again. "This may be a short-term job, but I really need the help. I'll pay you extra if you'll stay on the job twenty-four-seven."

"Double my pay on weekends," she suggested.

"Done," he said, nodding. He would have agreed if she had demanded that he quadruple it. Money wasn't the problem here. He glanced at the little baby who slept so serenely and looked angelic, yet he knew that was a mere facade.

David's gaze shifted to Marissa Wilder, and he was unaccustomed to the feeling of losing control to a slip of a girl who, in her frou-frou dress, appeared to be all of twelve years old. And the dress looked like something no female past the age of five would want to wear. With the glob of makeup on her face, she was ready for the stage. But he didn't care if she wore feathers and pajamas and had purple hair. She knew how to take care of a baby, and he had a dim recollection of her family and her older sister Karen, so she wasn't a complete stranger.

"Now, at night, am I to get up with Autumn?" she asked.

"Yes," he answered instantly, and held his breath to see if she was going to refuse.

She nodded. "Of course, I'm giving up all my benefits, my health insurance, my 401—"

"Marissa, I'll not only triple your salary—which, by the way, I found out from your manager what you're making—but I will pay your premiums for health insurance and I'll put in whatever the store contributed to a savings plan," he said, deciding she had a mind for money as well as a knack with babies.

"Thank you," she answered, brightening. "That's generous."

"It is, but I'm desperate."

"Why did you want to take Autumn if it was going to be such a big deal to you?"

"It's a long story," he replied, "but I've told you the main reasons—I didn't think she should become a ward of the state and her mother should be able to take her very soon. It hasn't been twenty-four hours yet."

"Here comes Manny," Marissa said, and then smiled. "Hi, Manny."

"Hi, there, Marissa," he said, wiping his hands on his apron, wearing his customary white undershirt that revealed his bodybuilder's muscles. "Look at you. Aren't you cute today."

"Thanks, Manny," she answered, her dimple showing again.

"Hi, Manny," David said.

"Hi, David." Manny looked at the baby. "This is the baby from last night, isn't it?"

"Yes, little Autumn," David said, still marveling how news circulated in the small town. He pulled out his wallet. "Let me pay you for the chili and for the other guys' dinners."

Manny waved his hand. "Forget it. It's on the house. You earned a free dinner last night. The chili is on me," the man said gruffly.

"Thanks, Manny, but you don't need to do that."

"Forget it. Did you see me on the tube last night?" Manny asked.

"No, I missed that. I was probably still at the hospital."

"Yeah. I got interviewed by a Midland station, too. Wanted to know all about the woman and baby."

So much for keeping a low profile, David thought. "How did Midland pick up the story?"

Manny shrugged muscled shoulders. "You know how news gets around in this part of the world. How's the mother?"

"I don't know," David replied. "I'll probably go by the hospital this afternoon."

"Yeah, well, hope she recovers real quickly. It's good you're helping her out. Good Samaritan Sorrenson. What are you folks having? I've got a breakfast special—eggs, grits, sausage, biscuits and gravy."

"Sounds fine," David said. "Okay, Marissa?"

"I think just eggs and toast for me," she replied.

"Aw, come on, Marissa. You need to put some meat on your bones," Manny urged. "I'll send out two specials plus some toast. You eat what you want." He turned and left, passing Sheila at the counter and giving her a pat on the behind.

Sheila giggled and sashayed away with platters of steaming bacon and eggs.

"Where do you live, David? You have a house in Pine Valley, don't you?" Marissa asked, mentioning an exclusive gated area in Royal.

"That's where my dad lives—when he's in Texas and when he's not traveling somewhere. Right now, he's out of the country. I live on our ranch, just west of town."

They talked about the job until Sheila brought platters of eggs, sausage, pale yellow grits with cheese and fluffy golden biscuits.

"I need to get some supplies for Autumn—she has very few clothes," David said, putting salt and pepper on his eggs.

"I can help you select some clothing," Marissa volunteered.

"Can we go back to the store from here and you show me what to get for her?"

"Sure. With your powers of persuasion, maybe you can talk my boss into letting me use my employee discount," Marissa teased.

"That's no problem." David waved away her suggestion. "You just pick out what we need, including diapers and a crib."

Marissa sat back and daintily wiped her mouth. David idly noticed that her mouth was delectable. He glanced at her platter.

"You didn't eat much," he said.

"I couldn't possibly eat all that. I only ordered eggs and toast."

"Yeah, well, Manny has never been known for small helpings. Ready to go?" he asked.

"Yes." She paused when he picked up the bill. "I can buy my own breakfast, David."

"You're my employee now, and I'll pay for your breakfast," he said, picking up the carrier. He glanced at Autumn. "She's sleeping better now than she did any time last night."

"She may be more relaxed now. Babies can sense when someone is tense, I think."

"Yeah, well, I was tense, all right, and so was she," David admitted.

They left the Royal Diner and drove back to the store, where Marissa made selections. David bought far more than she thought was necessary, but he insisted that he didn't want to have to come back and do this again. As soon as they finished making selections he arranged to have everything delivered to his house.

Outside in the parking lot, she turned to face him. "I'll go home and pack. Would you like to come meet my grandmother?"

"I'd like to and I will sometime soon. I don't want her to worry about your new job, but I have a meeting at noon and we shopped longer than I thought we would."

"That's because you almost bought out the store. Well, I'll be at your ranch at four o'clock."

He looked into her eyes, and he wondered if she had ever told a lie in her life. She didn't look as if she possibly could. Idly, he wondered how Grandma Wilder dressed. She couldn't be one degree more eccentric than her granddaughter. What was the house like? Visions of a gingerbread house danced in his mind.

"Okay, Marissa. See you at four. And thanks."

"You're welcome," she said, giving him one of her big smiles. She turned and walked away, pigtails bobbing and her full skirt and petticoat flouncing with each step. She wore some kind of striped stockings and what looked like pink ballet slippers, and he wouldn't have been surprised to see her start skipping to her car. Before he climbed into his vehicle, he glanced over his shoulder again and saw her behind the wheel of a very ordinary-looking four-door sedan.

"Well, little Autumn, you have a nanny now. One I think you like and whom I certainly like," David told the sleeping infant. "Tonight ought to be livable. Now, just keep sleeping, please. I have to go to the club to meet the guys, and babies aren't usually allowed in the clubhouse. You sleep through that and I'll buy you a rocking chair on the way home."

In minutes David parked in the Texas Cattleman's Club lot. The simple exterior of the clubhouse belied the elegant interior. With the carrier in hand, David entered the sprawling clubhouse, which was built in 1910 by Henry "Tex" Langley.

David strode through the familiar foyer, where walnut paneling was lined with oil paintings of past members. He continued through a lounge that held crystal brandy decanter sets, leather chairs, mounted animal heads and cases of valuable antique guns.

He finally entered a smaller room, reserved for their meeting. He was the first to arrive and settled down in a maroon leather chair, placing Autumn and her carrier on a chair next to him. Sunlight spilled through the long windows across the lush oriental carpet and over the pool table that stood on one side of the room. Along the opposite wall was a credenza holding another crystal brandy decanter set. A waiter quietly entered the room.

"Good afternoon, sir," he said, smiling at David. "Ah, and how's the little one?"

"She's fine at the moment, Jimmy."

"Can I bring you something to drink?"

"You might as well bring us some coffee and probably some pop."

"Fine. Anything else? Lunch?"

"Not for me. You can ask the others when they get here."

"Fine," the tall, graying man said, and left the room. No sooner had he disappeared through the door than Alex Kent came striding in. One look in his green eyes and David knew that Alex was bringing bad news.

Three

They shook hands, and Alex's solemn look disappeared as he eyed David. "Good grief, man! What happened to you?"

David rubbed his whiskered jaw. "I didn't have time to shave."

"Yeah, so I see. Try buttoning your shirt right, too."

"Oh, hell," David mumbled, looking down at himself. "I just grabbed something to put on."

"Rough night, huh? Did you have someone over and party after the wee one went to sleep?"

"Alex, you're pushing your luck now. Hell, no, I didn't party. I was up all night with her."

Alex leaned over the sleeping baby. "She's quiet enough now. I find it hard to believe that this little doll kept you up through the night."

"You want to trade jobs?"

Alex grinned. "Nope." He touched the baby's arm lightly. "She's a cute little thing."

"Yeah, well, it was a hellacious night. And don't you wake her," David snapped.

Alex grinned, turning to look at David. "Good thing it was you. I don't have a clue about kids."

"You think I know anything about them?" David demanded. "I just hired a nanny. Have you heard anything about the mother?"

"No, I haven't. Here's our man now."

Wearing the same clothes he had worn the night before and needing a shave, Clint strode into the room and shook hands with his friends. The waiter returned, bringing drinks and snacks, taking sandwich orders and then leaving.

With a long, purposeful stride, Ryan Evans entered and greeted them, and David shook hands with his quiet friend who, at thirty-two, was a few years younger than the rest of them. All the men clustered around the baby to look at her.

"I've got a nanny," David announced again for the others.

"You may need her for a while," Clint said solemnly as the men sat in leather chairs and David sat in a chair by Autumn.

Curiosity was in Ryan's brown eyes. "All right, guys, fill me in. Sorry I missed our usual chilifest."

"I'll bet you are," Alex teased. "Who was she this time?"

Ryan grinned and shrugged. "I had a good time. Now, what happened last night?"

"You missed a lot," David answered, relating the events starting with the woman's rush into the Royal Diner the night before. When he finished he asked, "Ryan, you didn't give this woman a Texas Cattleman's card, did you?"

"Me? No, I didn't."

"Just checking. You get around."

"I've been contacting members," Alex said, "to see if I can find who might have known her and given her the card. So far, nothing."

"I saw Manny this morning," David informed them, "and he told me about being interviewed for television last night."

"That was inevitable in a town this size," Ryan said.

"Anything unusual happens here and it's all over town within the hour, much less something happening in the Royal Diner."

"It'll pass, though," Alex remarked, taking a swig of pop.

David turned to Clint. "Now you need to bring us up to date on our mystery woman. Is she without a guard right now?"

"No, our Jane Doe has a guard. I called Aaron Black, and he said he could come into town and stay while I meet with y'all. He told me to take a few hours and get some sleep."

"Aaron's a good one to call," David said, thinking of the tall Texas Cattleman's Club member and fellow rancher.

"That's the great thing about our members," Alex said, stretching out his long legs. "They're always willing to help."

"That's what we all want to do," David added quietly. "Tell us about the woman, Clint. How is she?"

"Her condition doesn't look good. She's still in a coma. She's malnourished and dehydrated. She just gave birth not long ago and she's had a bad blow to her head," Clint replied.

"Thank goodness I hired a nanny this morning," David said, his hopes disappearing that the mother would be able to have her baby returned to her right away. He glanced at Clint, who had one jeans-clad leg propped up with his booted foot on his other knee. "What else?"

"She's in ICU and they told me they'll run tests all the rest of the week and probably into next week if she doesn't come around. They did an EEG, an electroencephalogram, to check her brain because there's some swelling."

"It doesn't sound good," Ryan said.

"We better say some prayers that she survives," Clint said, looking grimly at the baby. "That little girl can't lose her mother," he added, with worry in his blue eyes, and David was reminded of Clint's loss of his wife when fire claimed her life. Clint always seemed to have the hurt bottled up inside him, and David knew Clint carried scars from the fire. David looked down at the two crooked fingers on his left hand, knowing that he had his own scars. Perhaps every man in the room did.

"We have to do all we can for both of them," Alex said, bringing David's thoughts back to the problem at hand.

"The hospital is concerned. They're giving the mother a lot of attention, and we have an excellent staff here," Clint added.

"That's right," David agreed. "With all the wealth that people in Royal have poured into Royal Memorial, it rivals big-city hospitals." He shifted and looked at Alex. "Alex, what's your report? Any information on her identity?"

"None," Alex replied grimly. "There was a list of names in the bag she carried and I'll investigate them. This morning I checked with Wayne Vicente and there's no one on the missing person's report who fits her description. So far I haven't found out anything about her. Except one thing." His green-eyed gaze circled the room as he looked at each man. "She was carrying about half a million dollars in that bag. Most of it in large bills."

"Damn, that's a lot of money," Ryan remarked.

"I'd say it sounds like she's in a lot of trouble," David said, and the others nodded agreement.

"Half a million—what in blazes can she be mixed up in?" Ryan asked, and the men gazed at one another.

"Something dangerous," Clint said grimly.

They fell silent when Jimmy returned with more drinks and sandwiches on silver trays. Another waiter helped him, and in minutes, the men were alone. As soon as each had what he wanted to drink and eat, David returned to their subject. "Let's get back to business. Alex, go ahead with what you were saying."

"I haven't found anyone who remembers seeing her come into town. Not at the airport or the bus station. I don't have a picture to show anyone. I can only give them a description, but so far nothing. I'm just beginning to work on that list of names and dates she had in the diaper bag. Since she's malnourished, I'm guessing that the money hasn't been in her possession long. Her clothes were bought off the rack. Her nails aren't done professionally. If that money is hers, then she's one of those eccentrics who stashes every penny, but she's too young to accumulate that kind of money. My guess is that she's on the run," he said, and the others agreed.

"That means you need to continue to guard her if you can," David added.

"I can help out when y'all need me. I can spell you at the hospital, Clint," Ryan offered. He looked at Alex, whose thick brown hair was windblown. "I'll help you, too, Alex, if you need me for anything."

"Thanks," Alex replied as Ryan's gaze shifted to David.

"You're on your own with the baby, though."

"So I guessed," David replied with resignation. "When are Travis and Darin getting back?"

"I don't know, but we could certainly use their help," Ryan answered. "I'll get in touch with Travis and find out."

"So where do we go from here?" Clint asked.

"I'll keep trying to find out our mystery woman's identity and who gave her that card. I can ask here at the club and everyone will keep things confidential," Alex offered. "I put the money in the club safe and I'm staying in contact with the police chief." His green eyes twinkled. "So, David, you're our surrogate daddy. You just keep taking care of little Autumn. Looks as if she's happy."

"She is happy. She's got a nanny coming soon."

"Who's the nanny?" Alex asked.

"Marissa Wilder."

"I know her sister," Ryan said.

"Karen Wilder," Alex agreed. "I dated her once. She's a hoot. I think she was more of a party girl than her little sister. Karen's married now and has a passel of kids."

"So my nanny has a good background?"

"You didn't check?" Clint asked. "I can run a check on her background, but sounds like we've already got enough if you guys know her family. You didn't check on her?" he repeated.

"Hell, no, I didn't," David snapped. "If you'd been up all night trying to get formula down and a diaper on a baby and stop her crying, you'd snap up the first nanny you could find, too. Marissa has a knack with babies.''

"Well, so might have Lucrezia Borgia," Alex teased.

"You guys. Give me much flak and you can take this baby and then we'll see who runs out and gets a nanny," David answered, thinking about the night he'd just spent.

"Just keep it up, Dad. You'll do fine," Alex said. He rubbed his forehead. "Seems to me I remember Marissa Wilder being married."

"She's not married now," David said. "I asked her."

"Yeah, she was," Clint broke in. "A guy who was a doctor. After his divorce from Marissa, he and his new wife moved to Midland."

"I don't care if she's had five husbands," David said firmly, and the others laughed.

"I'm going," Clint said, standing and taking a last long drink of pop. Clint was as solemn as ever, looking worried and concerned. David was sorry Clint was mixed up in this because he didn't need any more hurt in his life.

"Frankly, David," Clint remarked, "you look like you had a rough night."

David merely waved his hand at Clint as if shooing away a fly.

Ryan stood. "I'll walk out with you, Clint."

"I better go while she's still sleeping," David said. "If she wakes and is hungry, they'll hear her all over this clubhouse." David picked up the new diaper bag and the carrier with the sleeping baby. She jumped, her tiny fingers spreading, and then she became still again.

"Looks like you have a peaceful baby," Alex said, falling into step with David. They walked out into bright sunshine. "I think we've got our hands full," Alex continued. "I just wonder where Jane Doe got that blow to the head. And who is trying to take her baby and why. It could be the father. Or relatives. I have a lot of questions and so far, no answers. Too bad that baby can't talk."

"She's vocal, just not into conversation."

Alex smiled. "You'll get the hang of it, and now you have help. From what I remember, the Wilders are a pretty good family. Her folks do some sort of charity work—I don't recall, exactly."

"She said they were out of the country. I think we know enough about the Wilders. Keep us posted, Alex."

"I will. The minute I find out anything, I'll let you and the others know. Jane Doe didn't pop into Royal from a void. And somewhere in her background there's someone from the club. I'll keep asking. And you keep up the great baby care. This will make you an expert so when you marry and become a dad, you'll know what to do."

"Yeah, right." David snorted. "Marriage has always been out for me—now I'm absolutely sure it's out. Growing up without a mom and my dad away half the time, I don't know anything about this family stuff."

"You're learning. You'll let all that knowledge go to waste," Alex teased. "What a shame."

"Yeah, right." David left his friend and hurried to his car.

"This car wasn't even made for a baby," David remarked to himself, struggling to get the new carrier buckled into the back seat. He looked down at the tiny baby, who still slept peacefully. He brushed her wispy hair with his fingers. "Darlin', you've been an angel. Now I'll live up to my promise and we'll buy a rocking chair on our way home."

As he closed the door carefully, he saw Clint approaching on his way out of the lot. David flagged Clint down, got the borrowed carrier and hurried to Clint's car, to ask him to return the carrier to its rightful owner at the hospital.

As Clint drove away, David climbed into the front, starting the engine and glancing into the rearview mirror at Autumn. "Sleep, little one," he said softly. "'Course, you're probably resting up for tonight, but that'll be between you and your new nanny. I'm going to hit the sack and pass out for twelve hours."

To David's relief Autumn continued to sleep through his purchase of a rocker and promise of delivery later that day.

Praying that she continued to sleep until he was home, he took the shortest route and sped home, finally turning from the county road onto his own ranch road. Iron gates were opened wide. Pipe-and-wire fencing ran up to two tall posts and a sign on one of the posts read TX S Ranch. He looked at the familiar TX S brand that made up the name. Stirring up a cloud of dust, he raced the car along the gravel drive.

He let out another sigh of relief when the sprawling house came into view. He loved the ranch. This was home, the happiest memories of his childhood had been here. In tight spots in far corners of the world, this was the place he dreamed about.

Made of sandstone, the house was built before the turn of the century in the late 1800s. David had often climbed up its shake-shingle roof, swung from the branches of the tall oaks that shaded the fenced yard and spent hours on the wraparound porch. Now the house was his haven from the world.

Beyond the house stood a barn, a bunkhouse, other outbuildings and a corral. In the distance several other houses could be glimpsed.

As he neared the four-car garage, a brown-and-black shaggy dog came tearing out of the shadows and ran to meet the car, jumping and wagging his tail, staying back a safe distance away from the car.

David parked and climbed out, idly scratching the dog's head briefly. "Now, General, you scoot. We've got a sweet baby who has come to live with us, and she's too little for you to play with."

Just then Autumn stirred and blinked, and for a few moments, gazed at the world in silence.

"We're home, little one. I'll have you changed and fed in no time. I'm getting to be an old hand at this," he said, hurrying into his house.

As he passed a rocker on his porch, he eyed it, and half an hour later he went back outside to pick it up and carry it into his spacious kitchen, which had a large living area at one end of the room. He picked Autumn up from her carrier and put

her on his shoulder, patting her as he crossed to the counter
to get her bottle he had just readied.

"Now, darlin', your diaper has been changed. We can rock
and you can eat and that ought to make you happy." He sat
down and shifted her carefully in his arms, holding the bottle
for her as he had seen Marissa do. In seconds Autumn was
happily sucking away and David rocked, marveling that he
had a baby to care for.

"I'm getting the hang of it," he said in amazement. "I'll
still be mighty glad to see your nanny arrive." He glanced
around the kitchen. His housekeeper, Gertie, had cleaned his
disastrous kitchen from last night. Imported tile countertops
were once again immaculate, as was the terra-cotta floor. He
looked around the room. It had rich fruitwood cabinets with
fruitwood covering the refrigerator. A workstation island separated the kitchen area from the living area, and one end of
the room held a large stone fireplace with a sofa and two
comfortable chairs. On the other side of that end of the room
stood a fruitwood oval table and twelve chairs beside a wide
bay window. Practical and comfortable with state-of-the-art
equipment, the room was one of David's favorite places. Now
the rocker was in the center of the living area.

David looked at the baby in his arms. Could he have ever
been this tiny? Before she died, in those early months, had his
mother rocked him? There was a rocker at the Pine Valley
house and it was old. He was certain his father had never
rocked him. He couldn't imagine his father dealing with a
baby. His father had always hired someone to do that job.

He glanced at the clock. Five until four. Would Marissa be
prompt? He didn't care, as long as she just showed up. He
had called home from the club and told Gertie to get a bedroom ready, that he had hired a nanny who was moving into
the ranch house.

He heard an approaching car and sighed with relief. When
the doorbell rang, David got up, careful to avoid disturbing
Autumn, who was still busily drinking from her bottle. He

carried the baby with him and swung open the front door, staring in amazement.

He wanted to ask, ''Who are you?'' Instead, he gazed into the same chocolate-brown eyes and saw the same delectable full lips.

Gone were the strange clothes and makeup. Before him stood a stunning woman who was all curves and long legs with a narrow waist. Shining dark blond hair fell in a silky curtain below her shoulders to frame her face.

Her skin was flawless, with only the faintest pink to her cheeks. She wore a simple blue cotton short-sleeve shirt that was tucked into a navy skirt. David reflected he'd be able to span her waist with his hands. He realized he was staring.

''You don't look the same,'' he blurted, and then wondered what had happened to his finesse.

She smiled, the same adorable, dimpled smile, only now it turned his insides to steam.

''No. I guess we never got around to discussing my clothing this morning. The store had a special sale going and they asked all the employees to dress as Mother Goose characters. I was Little Bo-Peep.''

''Bo-Peep?''

''You don't know your nursery rhymes—Bo-Peep who lost her sheep?''

''No, I don't.''

Marissa's brows arched, but she kept her comments on his lack of knowledge of nursery rhymes to herself. She looked at the baby. ''I see Autumn is doing just fine,'' Marissa said, and David realized they were still standing at the door; he was still staring, and he had not invited Marissa inside.

Hastily, he stepped aside. ''Come in. Are your things in your car?''

''Yes.''

''I'll help you bring them in. Let me finish feeding Autumn and then I'll show you around. I was in the kitchen feeding her. I carried a rocker in from the back porch,'' he said, wondering at himself. He was babbling—a first in his life. His mind reeled. He had hired what he thought would be a competent nanny. Now he realized he had hired a very appealing woman. How was he going to live with her under his roof and ignore her?

With one hand he pulled the rocker near the fireplace. Between the oval breakfast table and the fireplace was a plaid-upholstered sofa. He motioned toward the sofa. "Have a seat."

He sat as Marissa sat and crossed her long, shapely legs. He was in a sweat, and he realized he was staring again. He yanked his gaze up to meet her steady look.

"I bought a rocker on the way home today. It'll be delivered this afternoon. This one belongs on the porch and, frankly, I forgot I had it."

"Autumn looks more than halfway through that bottle. You might want to stop and burp her," Marissa suggested.

"Do what?"

"Little babies get air bubbles in their tummies when they take a bottle. Here, I'll show you. Where do you keep the kitchen towels?"

"In the third drawer by the fridge."

With a sexy sway of her hips that he could watch all afternoon, Marissa crossed the room, found a towel and returned to stand in front of David. "Lean forward slightly, and I'll put this over your shoulder."

He did as instructed and was acutely aware of her bending down to place the towel across his shoulder. He felt her hands flutter over him, caught a whiff of an enticing perfume that smelled a little like roses, and saw silky strands of hair close in front of his face. Her skin was creamy smooth. Damnation, he didn't want to be attracted to his nanny. That seemed bad business all the way around.

"Now, lean back and put her on your shoulder."

"I hate to stop her."

"She won't mind for a little while and she'll feel better. It might make her cry less if her tummy doesn't hurt."

He took the bottle from Autumn and set it on the floor

beside the rocker. He carefully put the baby on his shoulder and she snuggled against him.

"That's it," Marissa said, watching him. "Now, pat her back gently."

Marissa returned to the sofa to sit, and crossed her fabulous legs. He hadn't noticed her legs in those striped stockings this morning. Now he had to struggle to keep from staring at them.

Autumn gave a little burp that startled him. "She burped."

"Now you can go back to feeding her."

"I wish I'd known that last night," he said with a sigh.

"She probably wishes you'd known it, too," Marissa told him with a smile.

"You said you're not married, Marissa. I didn't ask about a boyfriend."

Her dimple flashed. "No boyfriends."

"A friend of mine said you used to be married."

Her expression didn't change, but David sensed he had touched a sensitive subject. "I was," she answered evenly. "To Reed Grambling. He's remarried and moved to Midland now."

"I knew him," David said, recalling a guy who was on the basketball team. "He was a year behind me in school and I remember that he was a popular guy. Sorry it didn't work out."

"I fell for his looks and charm, and beneath all that was a man purely interested in himself. And women. After I put him through medical school, he walked. He was through with me. But that's over, and I have my maiden name back," she replied.

"You had a rotten deal."

"I'm forgetting about it," she stated firmly. "Did you go by the hospital before you came home?" she asked.

"No, I checked with Clint Andover and there was no point in going to the hospital. Clint said the mother is still in a coma. She's listed as critical."

"How awful! Oh, my goodness, that poor little baby!" Marissa exclaimed, biting her lip and staring at Autumn.

''We'll all pray the mother pulls through this. In the meantime, Autumn is in good hands now.'' He looked down at the baby. ''She's asleep. If you'd like, I can give you a tour of the house.''

''Sure,'' Marissa said, standing when he did. ''This is a beautiful kitchen.''

''Dad had it done over several years ago. I was away in the Gulf War, so I didn't know until I came home. Some of the house has been remodeled and some of it is the original that was built when my great-great-grandpa Sorrenson settled here.''

Marissa listened to David's deep, husky voice, which was enticing all in itself. Was there a woman in his life? He had said there wasn't one to help with the baby. It didn't matter, she reminded herself. He was another man like her former husband—charming, handsome and interested in women who were beautiful and far more worldly than she could ever hope to be.

The house was spacious with large rooms, high-beamed ceilings and polished plank floors. David led her into a wide hallway, where oil seascapes hung along the walls and potted plants stood on the floor.

''Grandpa rebelled when he was young and ran away and joined the navy. He came home after a few years, but he never lost his love for the sea and he collected all these paintings.''

David took her arm lightly and steered her to the right. ''In here is the family room—this and the kitchen living area is where I spend most of my time.''

He dropped her arm, yet she could still feel the warm touch of his fingers and she was too aware of him at her side. Since her head barely came to his shoulder, he had to be a foot taller than she was. Tall, handsome, charming. As dangerous to a woman's heart as her ex-husband had been. Maybe even more so because she had thought David was cute since she was a kid. How was she going to be able to resist him? She was all but drooling on him right now.

Trying to focus on his family room instead of the man beside her, she looked at an enormous room with picture windows that gave a panoramic view of an expanse of ranch land. Bookshelves with books and pictures lined one wall. An immense stone fireplace had an oil painting of a schooner in stormy waters mounted above the mantel. A jumbo-size television screen was at one end of the room. A game table and four chairs stood in another corner. The ceiling was high with massive beams, and she wondered how much stone and lumber it took to build the house.

As she looked around, she suspected she was going to get to know too much about this sexy man—more than enough to fuel that old crush that had been dormant for so long.

They strolled through an elegant living room and large dining room with a long mahogany table that seated twenty easily. She saw the billiard room, the library, his office, and then they walked down the hall to the bedrooms.

"You'll be in this room," he said, leading her into a room with a four-poster bed and antique maple furniture. "I haven't considered where I'll put Autumn."

"Put her bed in my room if you want. I'll be up with her at night. Unless that's too far from your bedroom."

"Nope, my room is on the other side of yours."

"Oh, my!" she gasped.

His head whipped around. "Is something wrong?" he asked, looking at her intently.

"No, of course not," she answered quickly, feeling her cheeks flush. *In the next room.* How would she ever get a wink of sleep knowing that he was sleeping so close?

When she had driven to his ranch and had first seen the sprawling house, she figured she might see him only rarely because the place looked so big. But now she realized that wasn't going to be the case at all. He slept in the next room. There goes my sleep, she thought.

"Fine. The baby bed goes in here," David said cheerfully, unaware of the effect he had on her. "They promised to deliver it this afternoon." As if on cue, the doorbell rang.

"Give me Autumn and you can get the door," Marissa said.

Brushing his hands again with hers, he handed her the baby and left in long, springy strides.

She let out her breath. "Oh, my!" she repeated softly, and then looked at the sleeping baby in her arms. The little girl was precious, and Marissa couldn't wait to get her bathed and dressed in some of the things they had picked out at the store earlier.

She sat in a chair and cuddled Autumn, talking softly to her until she looked up and saw David standing in the door watching her.

"The crib is here," he said in his husky voice that held a peculiar, solemn note. "You can put her on your bed until it's set up. She can't roll off yet."

"I know. But I believe in holding and loving little babies. Even if she's asleep, I think she likes being held."

"She can't possibly know you're holding her."

"Oh, I think she does. And if she stirs, she'll know. This is more comfy than on the bed."

"I can't argue that one," he remarked dryly, and hauled an enormous box into the room. "I was going to put the bed up, but I don't want to wake her."

"You won't."

"I'll make a lot of noise," he said. "I may have to hammer."

"Babies can sleep through all sorts of noise," she assured him.

"I wish I'd known that last night," he remarked.

"Go ahead and set up the bed. If she wakes, we'll move to another room."

Marissa watched him work, noticing the play of muscles in his back and arms as he put the bed together. His hands were strong and well-shaped, except she noticed two of his fingers on his left hand were crooked and scarred and she wondered what had happened to him.

"I didn't sleep any last night, so after supper tonight, it's la-la land for me." He slanted her a look over his shoulder. "That okay? Can you manage by yourself this first night?"

"I certainly can," she said, watching the taut pull of his jeans over his long, muscled legs as he hunkered down to put the pieces together.

"Good! I've been dreaming of hitting the sack since midnight last night. And believe me, I'll be dead to the world. She eats every two hours or maybe more often than that."

"We'll be fine. You just go ahead and sleep," she said, thinking about him sprawled in bed, too aware that her pulse jumped at the mental picture conjured up by her mind. Knowing she better stop finding him so fascinating, Marissa still couldn't keep from watching every move he made.

Swiftly, he set up the crib and then left to find the bedding they had purchased together. In another few minutes he had a sheet on the mattress, a bumper pad secured inside and a mobile of colorful animals fastened to hang over the crib.

The next time the doorbell rang, he left and returned carrying a large, cherry-wood rocker. "I thought I might as well put this in your room. Where do you want it?"

"I don't know. Just set it down, and we'll figure out the best place later."

"If you'll give me the keys to your car, I'll bring it around to the back and unload your things."

"Sure." She fished in her pocket and held out keys, and his fingers stroked hers as he took them. It was the most casual touch, yet she tingled to the tips of her toes. He was gone again and back in minutes carrying boxes and suitcases.

He made three trips and then stood with his hands on his hips looking at her belongings. "You don't travel lightly, do you?"

"You didn't make it clear how long this job will last," she said pointedly.

He shrugged. "I didn't mean to question you about your things. I don't care if you move your grandma and sisters here and bring the entire household. I'm just so thankful to have a good nanny, anything you do will be fine."

"I'm here now, and she's a sweet little baby."

"When would you like to eat? If it's all right with you, we

can eat while she's asleep. And later, Gertie leaves. It'll be just the two of us.''

Just the two of us, spoken in his deep voice that all by itself was like a caress, sent another tingle spiraling in her. She hadn't been here two hours and she was having reaction after reaction to him.

''It doesn't matter to me.''

He looked at his watch. ''If Autumn is sleeping about seven o'clock, we'll eat, and then I'm bidding you adieu to sleep.''

''Fine.''

''I'm going to clean up, unless you want me to hold her while you unpack?''

''No. That's all right. She's asleep, so I'll put her down for a little while and get some of my things unpacked.'' Marissa moved to the crib, placing Autumn on her back. She stood looking at the baby, brushing her wispy hair with her finger. ''She's a beautiful baby.''

''She's a little miracle. I don't know how she put up with me last night,'' he said softly. He had moved to the other side of the crib, and Marissa looked up to see him studying Autumn intently. He touched her lightly with his large fingers. His skin was dark brown next to the baby's pale skin. ''She is pretty. I never thought that about a baby before, but then I've been around very few babies.''

''It was good of you to take her in.''

He looked up to meet Marissa's gaze. ''Her mother needs all the help she can get. And some prayers. These two are in deep trouble. Well, I'll leave you alone and see you at dinner. Holler if you want me.''

''Sure, David,'' she replied, and watched him go. I'm going to fall for him, she thought. Head over heels. He's sexy and handsome and he cares. She looked at the little baby again and experienced a rush of tenderness. ''Just think about the money,'' she whispered to herself. The money would help her fulfill her dream. A dream she had shared with no one else so far, and until today, it had seemed years away. But now, with the money she'd earn from David Sorrenson, she might be able to get her wish.

She touched Autumn's tiny hand tenderly and then she turned around to unpack.

When she went to supper, David had on a fresh navy T-shirt and jeans. With his hair combed and his jaw clean-shaven, he took her breath away, and he looked more like the David she had always known—only twice as appealing. She remembered him as a slender boy. He was a man now, muscled, tall, handsome. He flashed her a smile that revealed his even, white teeth, a winning smile that accelerated her heartbeat.

When he crossed the hall to her to take Autumn from her arms, she caught a whiff of aftershave. "Come meet Gertie," he said. "She made dinner and tomorrow morning she'll be back to clean and cook. All you have to worry about here is Autumn."

Marissa entered the kitchen and faced a tall, thin, graying woman who smiled broadly.

"Marissa, this is Gertrude Jones," David said. "Gertie, meet Marissa Wilder, our new nanny."

"Ah, that's good," Gertie said, smiling at Marissa. "And you like little ones?"

"I love them," Marissa replied.

Autumn stirred and began to cry, and the next hour was a busy one as Marissa changed and fed her and David hung around to help. Gertie offered to stay and serve dinner, but both Marissa and David reassured her that they could manage. As soon as Gertie was in the yard, David returned to the kitchen and locked up the house.

Supper was hectic, because Autumn woke up cranky even though she had just eaten and slept. Marissa and David took turns holding her and eating. Afterward, David cleaned the kitchen quickly and efficiently while Marissa soothed Autumn.

"I'm surprised Gertie doesn't want to care for Autumn," Marissa said as she rocked Autumn to sleep.

"Gertie knows as little about children as I do," he replied, drying his hands and crossing the room to kneel down and stack logs in the kitchen fireplace. "She lives here, just across the road on the ranch. Several employees live in their own houses. She worked for my dad. She's been here since long before I was born." As soon as he had a fire blazing, he turned. "Give Autumn to me and I'll hold her."

"I thought you were headed for bed to catch up on sleep," Marissa remarked, handing him the baby. David moved a few feet away to sit in a large leather chair, holding Autumn in the crook of his arm.

He shook his head. "Now that I know I can sleep, I'm not so tired. I want to get to know my nanny," he said, and she smiled, hoping he had no clue how simple remarks like that could send her pulse galloping. He tilted his head to study her. When she had been sixteen years old, she thought he had the sexiest eyes she had ever seen. As she looked at him now, she still thought so. His sea-green eyes with thick, black lashes had always fascinated her.

"You said there's no boyfriend. How do you spend your time?"

"With my family," she replied. "I take care of my niece and nephews. I take care of my sisters and grandmother. I jog and swim. Just ordinary things. What about you, David?" she asked. "Didn't you just get out of the air force?"

"Yep. Enough of that life," he said, stretching out his long legs and crossing them at the ankles.

"So now you'll take care of the ranch," she remarked, trying to keep her gaze from drifting down over him again.

"Not really. I'm taking some time, but eventually I'll move to Houston and go to work in my dad's oil company."

Marissa regarded his air of worldliness and could easily imagine him in a big city. In spite of his boots and jeans, he seemed the type more suited to city life than country life. But maybe that image had been conjured up by pictures in the paper of him with some socialite beauty on his arm.

"Are you going to live in Royal all your life?" he asked. All afternoon and evening he had given her his full attention and she decided he was a good listener. Too good, because he was very easy to talk to.

"I hope to always live here. I like being close to my family."

"So what'll you do with your windfall fortune if this nanny job lasts more than a week or two? What do you want?"

She thought of multiple answers she could give him, but then she saw no reason to avoid the truth with David. Their lives were touching only briefly, and then they would go separate ways and never see each other again.

"I haven't told my family, but I'd like to go to a sperm bank and have my own baby."

A twinkle came into his green eyes. "There are cheaper and easier ways—and more exciting ones—than to go to a sperm bank."

She laughed. "But other ways always mean getting involved with a man. I've done that and I don't want to do it again."

"I'm sorry that you got burned in that marriage."

"Yes, I did. While Reed went through medical school, I worked all six years of our marriage. As soon as he could stand on his own, he was off with another woman. And I found out that he was cheating on me almost from the beginning. So I'm not interested in dating again."

"You shouldn't lump all guys in with your ex."

"No. If I meet a real saint, I won't lump him in with Reed."

"A real saint is a pretty high standard," David remarked, looking at her so intently she began to regret revealing her deepest, most private wish to him.

"Well, a saint is about all I'm interested in, and the sperm bank sounds like the happy solution. What about you? You're still single."

He shrugged. "Marriage isn't for me. I didn't grow up in a house where there were good role models. My mom died when I was very young and my dad hired people to take care of me. Then I acquired a lifestyle that definitely wasn't for a

...ed man. Nope, no marriage in my future.'' He grinned. ''But I do like to date.''

She smiled at him. ''Well, I don't see another marriage in my life.''

His gaze trailed over her. ''I'd bet the ranch that you marry again.''

Her curiosity overwhelmed her. ''Why do you say that, David? You hardly know me.''

''You're too attractive to stay single.''

''Thanks, but loads of pretty women stay single. I think you date some of them.''

''True. But you look like the marrying kind. You love babies, for one thing. You like guys, for another.''

''I'm not touching that one. We really should keep things impersonal, sort of always on an employer-employee basis.''

His eyes gleamed. ''I thought that when you arrived, but now I don't know why we have to remain so businesslike. This may be a short-term employment.''

She shook her head. ''There's a good reason to keep our dealings with each other businesslike. I don't want another relationship. No, impersonal is much better. So what are your hobbies, David?'' she asked, growing hot beneath his blatant scrutiny and trying to get the conversation back to impersonal grounds, still too aware that he had just told her that she was attractive.

He smiled as if fully aware of her abrupt change in topic. ''I like to jog and swim and ski and do calf roping and go dancing with pretty women. You like to go dancing, Marissa?''

''Yes, with a saint,'' she replied, and his brow arched.

''A mere mortal won't do? Dancing's a pleasure. It doesn't have to lead to binding entanglements.''

''You know the old adage about playing with fire,'' she said.

''I think maybe you're missing out on some enjoyment in life.''

"And you're ready to fill in what's missing?" she teased, unable to resist.

He grinned. "Saturday night. Let me take you dancing."

"Whoa, cowboy! You're going way to fast. Like you did this morning. No dancing Saturday night, thank you," she replied, shaking her head but wanting to say yes instead. "David, I've been burned badly and I don't want any kind of relationship."

"I promise. Just a few hours of dancing. Think about it and I'll ask you again later," he said.

"Why do I get the feeling that you're very accustomed to getting what you want?"

"Sometimes," he said, giving her a level look, and she wondered when he *hadn't* gotten his way.

"For now, we're better off if we keep this situation very businesslike," she repeated firmly.

"Whatever keeps my nanny happy is fine with me." He shifted, placing one foot on his other knee. "What do your parents do?"

"They have a ranch near here for abandoned and mistreated animals."

"Wow! That's charitable. Is it a nonprofit business?"

"Yes. They have someone who runs the ranch for them. Actually, a staff of people. My parents spend most of their time either lobbying in Washington or on the lecture circuit."

"How did they get into saving animals?"

"Dad is a veterinarian. Also, he had some patents that caught on and that gave them the income to start the ranch. The ranch has taken most of their income. Because it's nonprofit, it's cost them a lot."

"That's commendable, I suppose," he said, and lapsed into silence.

"Want me to take Autumn now so you can go to bed and get some sleep?" she asked.

"That's not a bad idea," he said, coming up out of his chair with a fluid movement. She stood to take Autumn from him. He stood very close, gazing down at her.

"Good night, David," she said emphatically, and took Autumn, walking quickly away from him to the rocker.

"'Night, Marissa. Holler if you want me, but holler loudly." When he left the room, she wanted to wipe her hot brow. He was already flirting, and she could imagine that he saw her as an easy conquest and an easy way to pass the time and then go on his way and forget her. Too much like her ex-husband. David had said he had no intentions of ever marrying. No interest in commitment.

She did not stir the heart, soul and passion of men like Reed and David Sorrenson. She looked at the baby in her arms. No, she was the practical, somebody-to-rely-on-for-necessary-jobs person.

"Heart, stop beating so fast," she whispered. She had to summon more resistance to David Sorrenson. Especially if he hung around the house and flirted, because she knew he meant nothing by it except the most casual fling. Why had she told him about the sperm bank and opened herself up to suggestions? He hadn't come on so strong until after that tidbit of information.

She looked down at Autumn, who was blissfully sleeping. "Sweet baby, you've complicated my life, but I love you, anyway." For the first time she realized that she might have a double heartbreak. If she had this job very long, she would suffer when she had to give Autumn up, even though she wanted the little baby to be with her mother.

They fell into a routine, with David leaving early in the morning to work on his ranch and coming in at night. But as the days of the first week in November passed and moved into the second week, he began staying at home more, coming in earlier, leaving later in the morning, spending time with Marissa and Autumn.

Under the same roof with David, spending increasing time each day and evening with him, Marissa knew she was attracted more than ever to him. Moments together, casual contacts, all were building banked fires of longing in her that she ried to ignore, yet failed miserably. She found his smoldering gaze on her often and wondered what was running through his thoughts. He flirted, he charmed, he entertained her, and he was becoming more irresistible than ever. Yet she knew she needed to guard her heart against all that sexy charm and appeal, or she'd suffer the same hurt she had before.

Dodging sniper's bullets, David gritted his teeth and ran through the darkness across the uneven ground, away from the burning house that was a death trap. Even with the firefight going on, he heard the pistol shot ring out. Pain stabbed through him. He couldn't move his feet, couldn't breathe. He gasped for breath, wanting to scream, instead just gulping for air.

With a jerk, David sat up in his bed, disoriented for only a second, and then knowing he was in his room at the ranch, not halfway across the world, running for his life, having his heart torn out by the violent death of his best friend. He was sweating, the covers tangled where he had thrashed around during the familiar nightmare. He raked his fingers through his hair and studied the surroundings of his room, trying to get back to the world he was living in now and away from that hell that he couldn't shake out of his memory. Would the nightmares ever end? he wondered. Then he became aware of a baby crying.

He listened, stretching out again and putting his hands behind his head. Finally silence settled, but images of Marissa, only a room away, scantily clad in a see-through nightie, danced in his mind. Sperm bank. It was more than a week ago that she had told him about her secret wish, but he couldn't get it out of his mind. She shouldn't have to go that route at all. Not with her looks.

"Yeah, right," he said aloud in the dark. "Ready to volunteer?" he said to himself. He'd volunteer in a flash. She was sexy and appealing, and he knew there were times that he'd come on too strong, but he couldn't resist flirting with her. Yet he had better curb that flirting. If he overcame her reluctance and they started dating, Marissa was looking for a long-term relationship. And he would never marry. He didn't know how to deal with a family—except the way he was raised—and he would never do that to a wife or child. Some years he had rarely seen his father. That, and his dangerous lifestyle was still too close, too real. He was definitely not marriage material and Marissa definitely was.

Sperm bank—that was ridiculous. More images of Marissa in a nightie in bed in the adjoining room taunted him, and he turned on his side and closed his eyes and willed sleep to come.

After thirty minutes of tossing and turning he heard Autumn crying again and remembered what a time he'd had with the little baby the first night. He was tempted to go see if he could help, but he didn't want to set a precedent that he would regret later.

Why couldn't he sleep this past week when that first night all he had dreamed of was sleeping? And why had he put the baby bed in Marissa's room? Now if he went to see about Autumn in the night, he'd be in Marissa's bedroom. The thought made him hot.

Then the baby got quiet. Relieved, David stared at the ceiling while visions of Marissa in a nightie, rocking Autumn, plagued him. He tossed and turned for the next hour, finally falling into a fitful sleep. He stirred long before dawn, showered, dressed and left the house to pour himself into work.

Before going, he wrote a note for Marissa that he would return about six for supper.

"Get her out of your mind," he said, striding across his yard through the early morning darkness.

During the morning and early afternoon, he managed to get her out of his thoughts for a few minutes at a time and finally decided he was going home at three.

He made all sorts of excuses to himself, but deep down, he knew he wanted to see Marissa.

When he entered the kitchen, Gertie had supper in the oven, the table set and she had gone home.

"I'm home!" he yelled, hanging up his hat and coat and feeling his eagerness grow to see Marissa and Autumn. There was no answer, so he went to the family room. Finding it empty, he walked through other rooms.

He climbed the stairs and at the top of the staircase called to her again, "Marissa."

Wondering where Marissa and Autumn could be, he strolled down the hall. He was dusty from work and as he headed for a shower, he yanked off his T-shirt while he glanced into empty bedrooms.

Marissa's door stood wide-open and David knocked lightly. "Marissa?" he called. When no one answered, he stepped inside. Autumn lay on her back in the crib, sleeping, her tiny hands doubled into fists. Marissa was nowhere in sight. He crossed to the crib to look down at the sleeping baby.

"Hey, sweetie," he said softly, and heard a gasp behind him.

He turned and froze as he faced Marissa.

Four

He had been hot before thinking about Marissa. Now he was on fire. With her hair in a towel, Marissa stood wrapped in a large, navy bath towel, and his imagination ran rampant. The only thing beneath that towel was Marissa's warm, luscious body.

"You said you wouldn't be home until six," she said, the words little more than a whisper. She gazed back wide eyed at him. Under his steady, green-eyed scrutiny, Marissa was uncomfortably conscious of her state of undress.

"I didn't know you were in the house," she added, realizing she should move, get some clothes, do something except what she was doing—staring at him.

"I called and knocked on your door," he said, but she was barely aware of his words.

He was shirtless and she couldn't keep from staring at his muscled chest, which was sprinkled with curly black hair that tapered in a line to disappear into his jeans that still had the top button unfastened. The man was all solid muscles and tanned skin and sexy, male perfection. Her mouth went dry and her heart pounded. He was sinfully appealing.

As he crossed the room to her, she looked up to meet his gaze, which had unmistakable flames dancing in it. He stopped only inches from her.

She couldn't breathe, couldn't swallow, couldn't talk. Why had she taken this job? She hadn't been here long and already she was turning to mush. Worse, he hadn't touched her and she was melting. But the way he was looking at her would make any woman melt.

"Autumn's asleep now," he said in a soft, husky tone.

"Yes, she is," Marissa whispered as his gaze dropped to her mouth. "I have to get dressed—"

"Marissa," he interrupted, his voice dropping a notch deeper. Stepping closer, he slipped his hand behind her head, pulling away the towel that was around her hair. Thick locks of her dark blond hair spilled over her shoulders while his fingers wound in them and every touch stirred tingles.

With David's hands on her, she couldn't move away from him. All she could do was look into his eyes and see desire, a need for her that overwhelmed her.

"Move back, David," she whispered finally, certain he could hear her heart drumming.

"Why? A kiss is inevitable."

"No, it's not," she argued while her pulse raced. "Not while I'm standing here in a towel."

"We could remedy that," he said, and she clutched the towel she had knotted around her.

He hadn't moved and stood looking at her with that hot, hungry gaze that immobilized her. He leaned down, and his lips brushed hers so lightly, a feathery touch, yet it was a flame. "David, we shouldn't..." she whispered, trying again to find some resistance to him.

"Why the hell not?" he asked. "Don't tell me no when you want to. I can see desire in your brown eyes. Ah, Marissa," he drawled softly, "we've been headed this way since I opened my door to you."

I've been headed this way since I was eleven years old, she thought, unable to put up any more argument.

He leaned close again, his mouth settling on hers, and Marissa knew she was lost. And for a few minutes she didn't care. Stop him in a while, she thought. But for now, she was going to satisfy a lifetime of curiosity about the man. How many times she had dreamed of this moment! How many times she had imagined his kiss, fantasized that he noticed her, wanted her. This was something she had wanted too long, too badly to say no to instantly. Enjoy the moment, she told herself, and then the thought dissolved, replaced by feeling.

David slipped his arm around Marissa's waist, moving closer, his tongue touching her lips and then sliding into her mouth, stroking her tongue. She tasted sweet, hot, a golden torment, and a satisfaction that settled in his heart in a way he could never have imagined would be possible. She was a softness in his life that had been hard and harsh and on an edge. Yet here was sunlight, warmth, a woman to savor.

He tightened his arms, his kiss trying to devour his discovery, a blinding moment that transformed and shook him to the foundation of his being. Her softness was a promise of warmth that he had searched for as far back as memory stretched.

Marissa slid her hands across his sculpted chest, which was hard with muscles, coarse chest hair tickling her palms. Her hands went over his strong shoulders, feeling the slight ridge of scar tissue along his left shoulder, and then she wrapped her arms around his neck. Her toes curled, her heart pounded and her willpower crumbled.

When she wound her arms around his neck, his arms tightened around her and his kiss deepened. She kissed him in return, the roaring of her pulse drowning out all sounds, fiery tingles spinning inside, her world and her senses turning upside down.

She stood on tiptoe, past fantasies firing her kiss. David's kiss was all she had dreamed of and so much more! She had opened Pandora's box today and trouble of every kind was cascading down on her, yet what delicious trouble for the moment!

Feeling his reaction to her body and her kiss, she trembled, clinging to him.

This was David Sorrenson kissing her. David—man of dreams, girlish and otherwise.

He raised his head slightly. "Marissa," he whispered, and then he ducked down again, his mouth covering hers, his kiss as hot and passionate as the one before.

He bent over her, his fingers winding in her hair, his one arm still tightly banding her waist. She continued to return his kiss as need escalated, a sweet torment. She knew she should stop, yet she knew she couldn't stop. She had waited a lifetime for this moment and it had been worth the wait. Dreams burst into spectacular life.

Never had a kiss been like this. Never before had a kiss made her tremble, turned her insides instantly to jelly.

He had brought her into a world of fireworks and thrills. She tangled her fingers in his thick, soft hair, felt the warm column of his neck. She wanted to run her fingers across his marvelous chest, to make him react to her the way she was reacting to him.

As she stood on tiptoe and held him, she kissed him back, putting all she could into her kiss. And then, as if coming out of a fog, she realized what she was doing. This was the rush to heartbreak, to falling for another man who didn't take relationships seriously.

Clutching the towel around her, she pushed lightly against his chest, feeling his rock-hard muscles, wanting just the opposite of what she was doing.

Gazing intently at her, he backed away. The hunger in his green eyes made clear how much he wanted her, and his breathing was as ragged as hers. He ran his hand from her neck, down her back to her waist, and she was too aware that she wore only a bath towel.

"We have to stop now," she whispered.

"Maybe," he answered, stroking her cheek. He picked up

tendrils of her hair and wound them in his fingers, and her scalp tingled from the faint touch. "It's just kisses, Marissa," he said. "It's exciting to get to know each other."

"It's safer to avoid getting to know each other very well."

"Safer?" His brows arched. "Don't take life so seriously. You liked being kissed and I liked it. Deny that one."

"I can't. But I don't want to get all involved," she said, too aware she was standing arguing with him when she was almost naked.

"How about I promise that we won't. Just kisses, some good companionship. Where's the harm in that?"

"The harm is wanting more. Your kisses might be addictive." She was becoming annoyed with him now. "You think there's no danger of either of us getting hurt or falling in love or anything that complicates life?"

"Absolutely not. Remember, you want a saint. I'm no saint," he answered lightly.

"Somehow that doesn't reassure me." She stepped back, sliding her hand down to his forearm. His hands dropped to her waist as they stood gazing at each other. "You're so sure you won't get hurt when I leave?"

"Past history tells me I'm sure," he said, his expression becoming solemn. "The last years of my life, I've avoided commitment because of the dangers I've faced. I've done that until it's a habit. I don't want commitment. You don't want commitment. So let's relax and enjoy each other's company and have a little pleasure in our lives."

"David Sorrenson," Marissa began, her temper spiking, "someday, whether you want to or not, you're going to fall in love. You can't always go through life starting relationships and then waltzing out of them. Sometime, somewhere, you're going to get your heartstrings snagged and then you'll see why I'm wary, why it hurts so much."

He traced his fingers along the top edge of the towel, across the soft rise of her breasts, and she inhaled, gasping for air as if the walls were closing in on her. "You're way too solemn.

Lighten up,'' he said quietly while his caresses were stirring her again and making her want to step right back into his arms.

She ran her fingers lightly over the jagged scar on his left shoulder. "How'd you get this?"

When his expression changed, she knew he had just shut part of himself off from her. "In the military. I was shot," he said brusquely.

She inhaled sharply, realizing how tough he could be and what risks he had probably taken. His terse answer led her to believe he didn't want to talk about what had caused his wound. It had broken through the spell he had wrapped around her in the past few minutes.

"I have to get dressed," she declared. "You need to go."

"Ah, give me one more minute," he said softly, and she knew he was going blithely on with his intentions just as he had the morning when he had hired her on the spot and gotten everything he wanted.

Slipping his arm around her waist again, he lifted her curtain of long hair and moved it to one side. When he trailed kisses across her nape, she closed her eyes. Her breasts tingled, an ache deep inside her increased, and she had a fiery need to turn into his arms.

With deliberation she stepped back and pointed at the door. "Now, leave my room."

His gaze drifted slowly over her, taking in every inch and setting every nerve in her body quivering. "If you insist," he said. When he kissed her, he had dropped the T-shirt he had been carrying. He scooped it up and gave her another lingering, hot look. "I'm going to shower. Looks and smells like you just did. We could have done it together," he added with a twinkle in his eyes.

"You're wicked, David."

With a cocky grin, he turned to saunter out of her room.

She rushed to close the door behind him as if demons were after her and felt as though her own little demon of desire was threatening to catch her.

Marissa moved around the room, getting dressed in fresh

jeans and a blue shirt, thinking about the past few minutes, remembering the most fabulous kisses she had ever experienced, wondering what David was thinking.

Breathtaking kisses or not, she had no intention of falling in love with him. He would be another heartbreak. He had made it painfully clear that he wasn't into commitment. She wanted a relationship and she knew she wasn't going to change. But what kisses! Her heart pounded as she remembered them. He was sexy and charming and he cared about Autumn, a baby he barely knew.

Could she do what he had suggested—lighten up on life? Go dancing, kiss, walk away in a week or whenever the time came and not care? She knew she couldn't. She sighed. He probably saw her as stiff-necked, fearful, holding out for a commitment. She didn't know how he saw her, but she couldn't stop being the way she was.

If they parted tomorrow, how long would it take for him to forget her—a day, two days, a week? On the other hand, now that they had kissed, how long would it take *her* to forget *him?* A lifetime, she suspected.

Marissa shook her head. Life wasn't fair. But it would be a lot more fair to her if she took care to guard her heart the way David did his. His was locked in the deep freeze and no one woman was going to get close to it.

In the past few minutes he had fixed it so she was in knots, and tonight would probably be dreadful. This past year she had been sleeping soundly night after night because she had gotten over the trauma of her divorce. And now she would have to do something to shut out memories of David's kisses. But not quite yet. For a little while she could enjoy the moment and remember. They weren't in love, and she wasn't in any danger yet.

"David," she whispered, pulling on her clothes and turning to comb her hair.

In the shower David washed his hair, letting his thoughts run free. He was going to talk Marissa into going out with him this Saturday night. He couldn't wait to get her all to himself.

"Slow it down, buddy," he told himself beneath the splashing water. He knew Marissa's whole intent would be marriage and he didn't want that. Why couldn't the woman just go out for a few dates? That's all.

The thought conjured up memories of her kisses, and the nether regions below his waist grew hot again, desire tormenting him as he remembered her soft body in his arms. The bath towel was too slight a covering, he had felt her warmth through it. When he had let his hand drift down to her waist, he had wanted to slide his hand beneath the towel, down over her bottom and back up. Just thinking about her, he was getting all hot and bothered again. David tried to shift his thoughts elsewhere to chores he needed to do on the ranch. Thoughts of cattle lasted about ten seconds until memories of Marissa nudged them away again.

She was so scared of getting hurt that she had shut herself away from the world. Her divorce was two years ago—that was plenty of time for her to get on with life. David sighed and shook his head. Why was he having such a reaction to her? He had dated dozens of beautiful women and he hadn't been all tied in knots by them.

Marissa was different from all those women. There was a down-to-earth manner about her, a deep sense of nurturing where Autumn was concerned, a practical, no-nonsense approach to life. And there were her kisses that had all but melted him into a puddle. He couldn't recall having as intense a reaction to any woman's kiss as he'd had to Marissa's.

With a groan he finished showering and toweled off, dressing in clean jeans and a fresh T-shirt, moving automatically, lost in thoughts about his nanny.

He wanted Marissa in his arms, in his *bed*. The thought revved up his temperature another notch and erotic images tormented him even though common sense told him that he would never get her into his bed without some promise of marriage. And that wasn't going to happen.

He thought about Ellen Drake, whom he had dated some since being home again. She was amusing, lighthearted, sophisticated, and she didn't take things seriously. Ellen wanted to have a good time and to be seen in the proper places with the proper people. He suspected Marissa didn't give a fig about such things. He ought to forget Marissa before he found himself caught in a sticky mess with a weepy female.

Memories still too hot to handle rushed into his mind and he knew he couldn't just forget Marissa or ignore her. He wanted to persuade her to go out with him, which he suspected would not be an easy task.

A saint was what she said she wanted. Well, he wasn't one. But since he had no intentions of getting deeply involved, why should it matter?

Marissa was ruining his sleep as effectively as Autumn had her first night with him. He'd thought he would have long, peaceful nights. Now every night, sleep eluded him, and he wasn't thinking clearly during the day. Females! Get a grip, he told himself. She was just a pretty face. If she went out with him, fine. If she didn't, fine. Two weeks ago he hadn't even known Marissa Wilder existed. Forget her.

"Right," he grumbled aloud, trying to ignore his eagerness to spend the coming evening with her.

All evening Marissa kept him at arm's length and David had another miserable, sleepless night. Tuesday he was up before dawn, putting on coffee,

When he heard Autumn crying, he fixed a bottle and headed toward Marissa's room. He knocked lightly on the closed door and heard her cheerful voice call for him to come in.

"Good morning," he said, swinging open the door. His gaze swiftly took in her jeans and red T-shirt that clung to her delectable figure. She looked as refreshed as if she had slept around the clock, but she had reacted intensely to their kisses, so he knew there had to be some effect. When he looked into her lively brown eyes, his body temperature rose.

"'Morning, David," she said happily. "Thanks for getting Autumn's bottle ready. I'll feed her in the kitchen."

He handed Marissa the bottle, aware of their hands brushing, wanting to wrap his arms around her and take up where they left off yesterday. Instead, he trailed into the kitchen after her and asked what she wanted for breakfast.

While Marissa was busy feeding Autumn, he left, heading for her bedroom, where he crossed to the closet to quickly peek at the size in one of her dresses and to look at a pair of her shoes. Before leaving the room, he paused a moment, glancing around the bedroom that had been a guest room all his life and a room he barely recognized now. Gertie kept the house tidy and spotless and that was the way David had always known it. Not so any longer.

The bedroom was filled with Marissa's possessions: everything from two pots of blooming begonias to books, from makeup to a clock. Pictures of her family adorned the dresser. He picked up a picture of a smiling couple and decided they must be her parents even though they looked younger than he would have guessed. Hats were hung on the bedposts and he could picture her in the Bo-Peep dress again. This room fit more with that image. He smiled and left, wondering if Gertie would be in a huff. He might have to pay her a little extra for dealing with Marissa.

When he returned to the kitchen, Marissa was sitting in the rocker with Autumn. While she fed the baby, he called his foreman, Rusty Bratton, to tell him that he wouldn't see him today. They talked about ranch matters for a while and then David replaced the receiver.

"You're not staying here to help me with Autumn, are you?" Marissa asked. "If you are, you don't need to."

"Nope." He poured a cup of coffee and crossed the room to sit near them. He tried to keep from staring at Marissa, but he liked looking at her. Her hair was tied behind her head with a red ribbon, and he wanted to go untie the ribbon, and run his fingers through her silky hair.

She had put him off last week about a Saturday night date. He wasn't going to let that happen again.

"I'm going to town, so give me a list of anything you need or anything I should get for Autumn," he said.

"I'll do that before you go. I'd like you to pick up a Chutes and Ladders board game if it's convenient. My nephew Mitch will have his fourth birthday soon."

"Sure, that's an easy one," he replied, still thinking more about running his hands through her hair than the day ahead of him. "Get your list. I'm going to make some phone calls before I go," he said, and left the room before he did reach for her.

Less than an hour later, dressed in jeans, boots, a shearling jacket and a broad-brimmed Western hat, David left, glancing back over his shoulder to see Marissa standing at the window, holding Autumn close to her shoulder. She waved and he returned the wave.

In town after he had run his errands, David stopped by the hospital to talk to whomever was guarding Jane Doe. On Jane Doe's floor, nurses passed David with soft steps while farther down the hall, a door wheezed shut. He saw a familiar jeans-clad figure at the end of the hall. Clint nodded in greeting and came toward David.

David shook hands with Clint. "I had to come into town and I thought I'd stop to see if there's any change."

"Nothing," Clint replied, glancing at his watch. "Ryan will relieve me soon. And I talked to Alex and he still hasn't come up with any significant leads on her identity or the money. The police don't have anything on the missing persons list, either, that fits her description. No change. No progress."

"Damn, that's bad."

"How's the baby?" Clint asked.

"She's fine. She likes her nanny and vice versa, so no problem there. So there's nothing?"

"There was one little incident that might not have anything to do with Jane Doe," Clint said, rocking back on his heels with his hands jammed into his pockets.

"What was that?" David asked.

"Ryan was on watch in the early hours of the morning today. He went to the pop machine and was out of sight of her door for maybe less than a minute because it's right down there a few yards," Clint said, pointing behind David. "When he stepped back into the hall, a man was almost to her door. When Ryan appeared, the guy turned and left in a hurry." Clint shrugged. "It may mean something and it may have been sheer coincidence. Had it happened in the middle of the day, Ryan wouldn't have thought anything of it."

"If someone who's searching for her has found where she is," David said, "that's not good news, either."

"I agree with you, but we may be jumping to the wrong conclusion."

"Under the circumstances, you guys take care," David urged, glancing down the hall and seeing nurses and aides bustling in and out of hospital rooms. Two visitors strolled along the hall, looking at room numbers and disappearing into a room.

"We'll be careful and we'll keep watch over her," Clint promised.

"Can I do anything?"

"Nothing besides taking care of the woman's baby," Clint replied. "That's enough."

"I'm heading back to the ranch now. I hope something changes here or someone learns something. Our Jane Doe didn't just come out of a void. Someone must be searching for her. Someone must know her."

"Yeah, there may be a lot of someones."

David nodded and left, striding through the hospital and to his car with an uneasy feeling. The minute he stepped outside, he looked at his surroundings. His skin crawled as if he were being watched, yet he knew that was probably a foolish feeling. Still, his basic instincts about danger had protected him often in the past.

He sat behind the wheel of the car and waited, his gaze searching the hospital grounds and parking lot as he watched for anything unusual. People came and went in the most ordinary way. Finally he switched on the ignition and left.

It was late afternoon when David returned home. Marissa was in the family room on the floor changing Autumn, who was lying on a blanket. As David passed the open door, he called a greeting. His arms were ladened with boxes, and for a few minutes she could hear him making more trips to his car and returning with sacks. Then Marissa heard him talking to Gertie in the kitchen.

Finally he came into the room, his green gaze meeting hers with the force of a blow. She was breathless, staring at him, reacting to nothing more than his gaze, but that was enough. The navy sweater and jeans complemented his black hair, and made him look very sexy.

Knowing she shouldn't stare, Marissa turned to pick up Autumn. When she did, David crossed the room to take the infant from her. "Let me hold her for a little while. I missed both of you," he said quietly.

"Did you get all your errands run?" she asked him, trying to ignore his remark about missing her. She smoothed her pale blue T-shirt into her jeans and then caught him watching her.

"Yes, and I got that game you wanted for your nephew," he said, mentioning the game she had on her list.

"I can't believe that you never played it," she said, recalling their discussion earlier. "You don't know some of the basic kid stuff. You didn't know Bo-Peep. What kind of childhood did you have?"

"Maybe not your run-of-the-mill nursery-rhyme-filled one," he said lightly, "but I had a childhood."

"I'm beginning to doubt it. I need to get Autumn a bottle," Marissa said, and David walked with her to the kitchen, which was filled with enticing smells from Gertie's afternoon cooking. Marissa's appetite had taken a nosedive, brought on by a running current of excitement over being near David, a condition she wished she could control.

"I'm through now," Gertie said, shedding her apron and getting her coat. "The table is set, everything is dished up and covered and ready. I'll go, unless you have anything else you'd like done before I leave.''

To David's amusement, Gertie said all this to Marissa without once glancing in his direction. How had Marissa become the boss in his kitchen when he had been in charge here for years now?

"No, thanks so much," Marissa said. "Anything else that you want, David?''

"Oh, no. Thanks, Gertie. We'll see you tomorrow.''

In seconds, she was gone, cold air wafting in from the door being opened. David stepped to the door to watch her walk to her house. He studied his surroundings until he was satisfied everything was safe.

Autumn stirred and Marissa took the baby from him.

"It's time for her to eat. If you're hungry and don't want to wait, go ahead without me.''

"I wouldn't think of going ahead without you," David drawled. "I've been looking forward to dinner with you all afternoon.''

"Oh, my!'' she sighed, giving him a wide-eyed look that made David's pulse jump. She reacted, all right. In spite of her protests and logic and caution, she responded to him. He drew a deep breath, glancing at Autumn and knowing they had to take care of the baby right now and flirting with Marissa had to wait.

"I'll get her bottle ready," he said, and left the room.

Marissa watched him, her heart racing over his words and the look in his eyes. Since yesterday, she had lectured herself to keep her guard up. Did she want another heartache like her divorce? She knew the answer to that one. Instinct told her that David would never be into anything lasting and she knew she would never be into anything casual.

When David handed her a bottle for Autumn, Marissa sat in the rocker, settling the baby and watching her take her bottle. David moved around, turning on music, building a fire, finally sitting down near Marissa.

"While you were in town, did you find out anything about Autumn's mother?" Marissa asked.

"I went by the hospital. Her condition hasn't changed."

"Oh, I'm so sorry! Poor baby and poor Mommy," Marissa said, tightening her arm slightly around Autumn, who was taking her bottle and watching Marissa with an intent stare.

"I don't suppose they know any more about your Jane Doe's identity," Marissa said. "If they did, I'm sure you'd tell me."

"That's right. Every search is a dead end, and no one has popped up on missing persons lists who fits her description. It's still a puzzle. She has to have family somewhere."

"Maybe not. Not everyone does."

He shrugged. "There are times and places I've been completely out of touch with my family, so if something had happened to me, no one who knows me would have learned about it for quite some time."

"I don't know how you did that kind of work. Or why."

"Maybe to avoid the regular job that is waiting for me in Houston," he replied, raking his fingers through his thick black hair. "When you're young, right out of college, life looks different. At the time, I didn't want to sit in an office day after day."

"And you do now?"

"I'm resigned to it more than I was then."

"Resigned?" she asked, surprised. "Why are you doing it if you don't want to?"

"I've been aimed that direction all my life with a detour to the air force. Dad expects it of me, and there's no big reason to disappoint him. That's not my habit. I figure I'll get used to it."

"That's a dutiful son," she remarked, seeing another side to him. "It'll be different from what you've been doing." All the time he answered her, Marissa was aware of his rugged handsomeness. She probably should have avoided this job and David Sorrenson at all costs. But then she glanced down at Autumn in her arms, and warmth for the baby filled her. The job was fabulous pay and the baby was adorable. She should just guard her heart no matter how sexy he was.

"I pray your Jane Doe recovers soon so she can get her baby back. Autumn's a wonderful little girl, David."

"I'll bet you say that about every baby you've taken care of," he said, smiling at her.

She smiled in return. "I might have."

Crossing the room to the wine rack, he held up a bottle. "Want to celebrate? Want a glass of wine?"

"Fine. After Autumn is fed and asleep. What on earth will we celebrate?"

"That you've become Autumn's nanny."

"Good enough," Marissa responded, laughing, a tiny inner voice telling her that she should have refused the wine, should stop chitchatting with him, should keep this all business. Even as she argued mentally, her inner voice was losing the battle.

In the living area of the kitchen, David stoked the fire. Then he finished getting dinner on the table and took Autumn for a time until finally the baby was asleep and he put her to bed.

The moment he walked back through the kitchen door, his gaze met Marissa's, making her breath catch. Watching her, he brought a glass of wine to her and held out his in a toast, his riveting gaze still on her. "Here's to little Autumn coming into our lives."

"That's reason for us to celebrate, but I hope her mother recovers soon."

"I do, too. But I'm glad we met," he said, his voice lowering, giving her a thrill she knew she should be wary of.

David touched her glass lightly and watched her over the rim of his while he took a sip. She drank the red wine, thinking nothing could be as heady as the desire she saw in his green eyes.

"Ready to eat?" he asked in a coaxing voice, as if he were asking her something entirely different.

When she nodded, he took her glass, setting it on the table, and then held her chair for her, his hand grazing her shoulder lightly, yet a contact that she felt to her toes.

David sat facing her, and as she looked at him across the table, she remembered dreams of girlhood. Now here she was, living in his house, having dinner with him, and had exchanged passionate kisses with him. It's just a temporary job, she reminded herself.

He passed her a platter with thick slices of roast beef. "Roast beef, potatoes and gravy are Gertie's specialty. You've won her over. I'm not sure she remembers I live here."

"Don't be ridiculous. She's just very friendly."

"She was as thankful to get you as I was. I was too distraught the first day to remember my name."

"I'm still surprised at that. A baby is simple."

"Not to me. Where babies are concerned, I'm green as grass, as you well know by now."

Marissa bit into tender roast and chewed. "This is delicious." She tilted her head to study him, wondering about his life. "How come you don't know Bo-Peep or the game I asked you to buy today? Did they keep you locked in the attic?"

"No. My mother died when I was a baby. I was raised by a very fine man who knew little about children and didn't care to get to know much about them. He hired nannies and tutors and sent me to school and took care of my needs and I did what was expected of me, but there are big gaps in my childhood background. I didn't do a lot of playing like some kids did."

"You weren't exactly lacking," she said, glancing at his surroundings.

"We always had material things," he said, shrugging, then continued. "Dad inherited money and made still more money, but I just kept quiet, did as I was told, and enjoyed myself in my own quiet way. I loved to read and play soccer and swim. I played tennis, too. Later, I played football. I kept busy, but whoever my nannies were in the early years, I guess they weren't into cute games and nursery rhymes. There were so many of them, I can't even remember them until I was about six. Gertie was always around, but she's not into kids any more than my dad was. Still, she was good to me and slipped me treats whenever I wanted them.''

''What about other relatives?'' she asked him, thankful she'd had the childhood she'd had, thinking about her sisters and her other relatives.

He shrugged. ''I have my grandparents, who are not into kids, either. Even less than my dad. I suppose it's passed from generation to generation.''

''Surely not!'' Marissa exclaimed, her brows arching. ''You've done quite well with Autumn.'' She sipped her wine and took another bite of roast beef. ''Don't you want to marry and have a family?''

''With my career in Special Ops, I scratched marriage off the list when I went into danger. That's no life for a married man.''

''I thought you were through with that now,'' she pointed out, buttering a fluffy roll and taking a bite.

''I'm through with the military, but I'm older, set in my ways, and don't know anything about a happy marriage or family life as you know it. I'll probably stay single,'' he replied, and Marissa wondered how many broken hearts he had left in his wake. ''Maybe someday '' David said. He paused to eat and then said, ''I'm getting the hang of baby care with Autumn. She's a lovable little thing. Maybe I'm seeing her through your eyes.''

''No, you're not! You haven't known me that long.''

''You make your personality felt. When you were growing up, I'll bet you played all sorts of games and had all sorts of kids around,'' David said, watching her and imagining her life, which was a contrast to his.

''You're right,'' she said, giving him a dimpled smile. He touched her cheek.

''Your smile makes me want to smile.''

Marissa warmed to his words, but didn't want to. As far as resisting him, on a scale of one to ten, she knew she was definitely one.

As they continued eating a long, leisurely dinner, they

talked about their lives. She learned a little more about his background, listened to him talk glowingly about the ranch, and she realized he was a cowboy at heart and loved ranching.

She was unaware of time passing, but finally he pushed away from the table. "We're finished, let's move to the sofa."

"We should clean this up."

"That's what I pay Gertie to do. Just leave everything and come here." He held her chair and then took her arm, leading her to the sofa.

Too aware of his fingers lightly touching her arm, Marissa felt her heart race, and she had a silent argument with herself whether to sit down beside him or move away to a chair and keep some distance between them. While she debated, he stopped and faced her. "Now, close your eyes. I brought you a surprise today."

Five

"**A** surprise for me?" Marissa asked, startled. "David, you barely know me!"

He framed her face with his hands and her heart thudded as she gazed up at him. "I intend to know you better," he said, his honeyed voice escalating the reactions to him that she had already been having. His hands were warm on her face while his expression showed unmistakable desire. Her lips parted and she drew a deep breath, finding it difficult to get any air.

Torn with conflicting emotions, she caught his wrists. "This is a job. You're my employer. David, we should keep this businesslike."

"Give me one good reason," he said quietly.

"So one of us doesn't fall in love and get a broken heart."

"Are you ready for a serious relationship?" he asked.

"No! That's what I'm trying to tell you!" Marissa exclaimed. "I trusted my ex-husband completely, and he used me and broke that trust. He was unfaithful and I don't think he ever intended to stay married. He was just waiting while I worked to help put him through medical school. Right now, I don't want to get involved with anyone again.''

''I don't, either,'' David replied. ''That makes us immune to hurts. Just relax and lighten up. You were hurt, you need to get out and live a little, and some of the hurt might go away.''

''You should be in sales,'' she said dryly, wondering if he was more than barely listening to her. ''That's the argument of someone who's never been hurt.''

''I've never been through divorce,'' he admitted, ''but you can't shut yourself off from life. Not you. You're too filled with life yourself to withdraw from the world.''

''Argue all you want,'' she said with exasperation, too aware of his thumbs moving lightly on her cheeks. ''I've had enough experience with getting hurt and I know what I'm talking about.''

''You'd think I'm getting ready to propose. This is no big deal. Relax and enjoy yourself. I don't think you've done that for a long time. Now, close your eyes, Rissa,'' he instructed softly.

The nickname was a lick of fire along her veins. No one had ever called her Rissa or any other nickname. Said in his husky voice, it was special, filling her with warmth. She took a deep breath and closed her eyes.

''I'll be right back. Keep your eyes closed.''

She never heard him leave, realizing he could be very quiet when he wanted, but she knew when he stopped touching her. Why did she have such an intense reaction to the man? Why couldn't she see him like she saw other men? Her excitement grew, more over David than over possibilities of a surprise. *Why* was he giving her a surprise? He had continually caught her off balance from the first moment she had looked across the counter into his green gaze.

''All right, open your eyes.'' He stood in front of her holding a stack of boxes. ''These are for you. Open the big one first,'' he suggested. ''Then the others make more sense.''

Conscious that he stood nearby watching her, she moved aside smaller boxes and lifted the lid on the largest box. Shuffling aside layers of tissue paper that crackled to the touch, she held up a lightweight black wool dress. It was slim, tailored and beautiful. "David, it's gorgeous!" she exclaimed, and then realized all the implications.

"I can't take this!" she gasped, turning to look at him. "This is a bribe, David Sorrenson!"

"Of course you can take it. It's yours now. It's not something *I* want," he added dryly. "And it isn't a bribe. It's a gift."

"You know I can't take this. Sneaky and underhanded is what I'd call this," she said, feeling as if she were drowning in his persistence and her own needs, knowing she was hurtling headlong into hurt with every moment they were together.

"Sneaky and underhanded sometimes gets you what you want. Now, stop arguing. It's yours. Wear it with me Saturday night. I want to take you out. The Texas Cattleman's Club has dinner dances twice a month on Saturday night. I want to take you to this one. Now, open your other presents."

"You'll go to any lengths to get your way," she muttered, exasperated and delighted at the same time. He was coming on too strong, too fast, and she was too attracted to him, too susceptible. "Absolutely—"

He placed his fingers lightly on her lips. "Shh. Think it over before you disappoint both of us."

He stepped close, sliding his hand around her waist and tilting her chin up to look down into her eyes. "As to going to any lengths to get my way—guilty as charged. Especially when what I'm after is a beautiful, sexy woman who has ruined my sleep and is driving me wild with her arguments. Wear the black dress and go out with me," he coaxed softly in a seductive voice. "Let's go out Saturday night."

"What about Autumn?"

"I already have that taken care of," he answered.

"How can I say no to that?" she whispered, lost in the depths of his gaze.

"Good!" he replied, taking the dress from her hands and tossing it on a chair. He leaned down to switch off the lamp, leaving only the flickering light from the fireplace and the light in the other part of the kitchen behind them.

Her breathing altered as he straightened, letting his gaze drift down to her mouth. "I've been waiting since yesterday, Rissa," he whispered.

"I know I should say no to you."

"Never," he whispered, trailing kisses along her throat and over her ear. She inhaled deeply, looking at him so close. He was clean-shaven, his thick raven hair neatly combed.

"David, listen to me," she protested, placing her hands on his forearms, a tactical error because every physical contact turned her brains to more mush.

"You listen to me," he whispered, brushing her lips lightly, so tantalizingly, with his.

She could barely listen to anything except the thunder roll of her heart. "No, no and double no."

"Yes, yes and triple yes," he replied. "There's no good reason to avoid a few hours out together, a few hours of dancing, good food and companionship, that has us both relaxed and content. Deny that one, Rissa."

How could she deny him anything? "I'm lost," she whispered without thinking. "Hopelessly."

"Ah," he said. Vaguely, she heard the satisfaction in his voice and knew she was defeated. How could she persist in a fight about going out with the man she had dreamed of having a date with for years?

His mouth possessed hers, his tongue stroking and playing until the blinding spiral of heat tightened and burst into searing longing. He had stormed her barriers and won the battle. She couldn't resist. She wrapped her arms around his neck and returned his kiss, snuggling against the solidity of him and hearing a groan caught deep in his throat.

"You dirty fighter," she whispered, coming up for air and running her fingers through his hair.

"If I win, it's worth it," he answered, and then his mouth covered her reply and her battle ended. With a thrill she felt his hard length pressed against her, her thighs against his muscled thighs, her breasts against his sculpted chest.

While he caressed her nape with one hand, his arm held her tightly. Their breathing became ragged; his kisses deepened.

She knew she was playing with a fire that sooner or later was going to burn her to cinders, but she couldn't stop. Not when his heady kisses melted every impulse to resist.

His hand slid down her back, and then he tugged her T-shirt out of her jeans and slipped his hand beneath her shirt. His hand was warm, callused, delightful. While fiery tingles increased, his hand slid around to cup her breast.

She gasped as new sensations shot through her, heating her further, driving her wild. When she pressed her hips against him, she felt his hard response to her.

He tugged away her T-shirt and flung it aside, unsnapping her wisp of a bra and pushing it off her shoulders. Then he cupped her breasts in his large, tanned hands, his thumbs circling and caressing her taut nipples.

She cried out, holding his strong upper arms, closing her eyes and immobilized by nerve responses that streaked from his touch. Trembling, she grasped him, wanting him, wanting everything, knowing she shouldn't be wanting any of his loving.

Enjoy the moment danced through her mind. Just for a time. A time to lose her heart completely. She slipped her hands beneath his sweater, running her fingers through coarse chest hair, over his hard muscles, stroking his nipples and hearing him groan again, a sound lost in their kisses.

In seconds, he tugged his sweater over his head and tossed it away, pulling her close against him while he continued to kiss her.

She caressed his smooth back, wanting to touch and be touched, unable to believe that this was David who was kissing her and wanting her to go out with him. How many dreams had been spun around him, how many nights of fantasy! Now he was here, his strong arms around her, and he wanted her. He was wicked temptation and irresistible desire.

His hands were at the belt of her jeans when she realized where they were headed. She caught his wrists in her grasp, twisting slightly to look up at him.

"David, you have to stop. You're going way too fast," she gasped, melting under his gaze.

"You're beautiful, Rissa," he whispered, stepping away slightly.

Quickly, she picked up her T-shirt, yanking it over her head. As soon as she pulled it down, she again met his smoldering gaze, which was as potent as a caress.

His jeans bulged with his evident arousal, and he reached out to stroke her cheek. He stepped close and pulled her into his arms to kiss her again.

Even though Marissa intended to push him away, she wrapped her arms around his neck. David leaned back to look down at her. "Come out with me Saturday night," he rumbled. "Say you'll go."

"I'll go," Marissa said finally. "But let me catch my breath. You go far too fast for me, David."

Suddenly he grinned, an infectious, white-toothed grin that dazzled her.

"Yee-ha!" he exclaimed, throwing back his head and letting out another whoop. "We've got a Saturday night date!"

She couldn't keep from laughing. "You browbeat me into it."

"You call that browbeating?" he asked. "I have another name for it."

"Seduction," she said. "Watch out, David. You're playing with fire."

"I'll be careful."

"I guess with a Special Ops background, you like risks and life on the wild side, but I don't. I don't want more hurt."

He tilted her chin up, lifting long strands of dark blond hair away from her face. "My last intention is to hurt you," he said, and his voice held such an unmistakable note of tenderness that it made her knees weak.

"Maybe, but that doesn't mean it won't happen," she replied. "And slow down with the seductive kisses, because I have no intention of finding myself in your bed."

"Is that right? I'll remember that. At the same time," he drawled, letting his hands slide down her arms and settle on her waist while his gaze drifted leisurely over her, "maybe my goal is to get you into my bed."

Marissa sighed. "Half of me thinks you're teasing and half of me thinks you're serious and both halves are right." She leaned over to snatch up her lacy bra and jam it into her jeans pocket. She turned to find him still watching her.

"Sit over there, and I'll sit over here and we can talk," she announced, trying to summon as much force into her voice as possible, knowing she was failing and he wouldn't care, anyway.

"Darlin', how about a compromise?" he asked, sweeping her into his arms and going to the sofa to set her down in one corner. He turned and sat in the other corner, twisting to face her and smile at her. "How's this? There's space between us, but I can still touch you a little." Stretching out his long arm, he caught tendrils of her hair and twirled them in his fingers.

He was too close if he was in the same room with her, but at least she had slowed him down enough that she could gather her wits. She tried to ignore the fact that her body ached and tingled and burned for more. She could happily drown in his kisses for the rest of the night, but she knew where that would lead and that wasn't what wisdom indicated she should do.

And that magnificent chest was still bare and still in touching distance. And far too distracting for a regular conversation. "Aren't you cold?" she asked him, giving his chest a once-over again.

His brows arched. "You want me to put on my sweater? My chest disturbs you?" he asked with great innocence.

"You know what you're doing," Marissa snapped. "Go

without your sweater. I can resist your chest," she added, and he grinned, snaking out his long arm to grab his sweater and pull it over his head. He raked his fingers through his hair and it sprang back in thick waves. Marissa knew it didn't matter a whole lot whether he had on his sweater or not because everything about him stirred her hormones.

"So if we go out—" she said.

"You said yes. *When* we go out—not *if,*" he reminded her.

"When we go out, who is taking care of Autumn?"

"I have that all worked out," he replied smoothly, his fingers caressing her nape as he shifted a few inches closer to her. "I have a neighbor and fellow Texas Cattleman's Club member and friend, Jason Windover, and his wife, Meredith. They have a little boy who was born in June of this year. We'll take Autumn to their house. Meredith is great, and Jason is ex-FBI so Autumn will be safe. How's that?"

"Ex-FBI? Autumn needs an FBI or Special Ops person around? Is she in danger?"

"She could be. No one knows because we don't know anything about the mother," he replied, letting strands of Marissa's hair slide through his fingers. She found it difficult to keep her focus on their conversation. Tingles and aches tormented her while her attention was drawn like a magnet to David, and even though his chest was covered by his sweater, she knew it was there, temptingly close to touch and kiss.

"But you do know something," she pressed.

"Yes, a little," he replied, and related all the incidents of the night Autumn and her mother came to town.

"Half a million dollars! David, someone is probably after that money!" Marissa tilted her head to study him. "Out of the goodness of your hearts, you guys are guarding her, caring for her baby, safeguarding the money and trying to find out her identity?"

"Something like that," he answered solemnly.

Memories flitted to mind, dredged up from the past as she studied him. "I remember some rumors about Texas Cattleman's Club guys helping people in trouble. It's true, isn't it, David?"

"That's what we're trying to do here."

"You don't have any idea how much danger Autumn is in?"

"No, we don't. Chances are, someone is after the mother and the money. Unless she kidnapped the child and took the money. Then that's different. But I think it's probably the mother who is in the greatest danger."

"Well, I'm glad you told me," Marissa said, wondering what she had gotten herself into.

"Don't worry," he said. "You're safe here on the ranch. I have alarms all around the house and the outbuildings. I have dogs."

"I met two of the dogs last week, and they're as ferocious as pudding," Marissa pointed out.

"They bark and they're good about strangers," David replied. "And I have six dogs on the place. The guys who work here have been alerted and Gertie is always cautious. My Dad wanted this ranch to be a shelter from the world and he started all this security stuff. Then, when I was in the military, I added to it."

"You might have warned me."

"You're not in danger, or I would have. Besides, I'm close at hand."

"*You* may be my greatest danger," she replied breathlessly, because he was lightly caressing her nape.

"I'm no threat to you," he replied blandly. "Wait until Saturday night and you'll see that all your fears were for naught."

"Right," she replied, suspecting she was going to regret her Saturday night date with him for a long time. "And regarding Saturday night. Will we pick Autumn up on the way home?"

"Yes," he replied, leaning a little closer and letting his fingers skim across her back and shoulders as he twirled long strands of her hair in his hand. "Or, Meredith said we can leave Autumn all night."

"No way. We pick her up," Marissa said firmly, trying to ignore the effect he was having just playing with her hair and lightly touching her. She was aware of each little tug and pull, aware when his hand stroked her. "Autumn is too little. I want to bring her back here." She did not add that she also didn't want the temptation of being alone with David.

He smiled. "I think I picked the best nanny in all of Texas. You'd think you were her mother."

"She's too little to leave with someone else all night long."

"I won't argue about it. As long as we have Saturday night, I'll be happy to pick her up. As far as leaving Autumn with someone else—she's here with us, instead of being with her mother, and she spent one night with just me, a totally inexperienced male, which was not the greatest for her. But if you want to bring her home Saturday night, that's what we'll do," he said, and smiled at her.

"Thank you. It's definitely what I want to do."

"She'll be in good hands, I assure you."

Marissa stood and picked up the black dress and held it up. "This is beautiful," she said. "You shouldn't have done that."

"I did what I wanted to do."

"I'm sure you did!" she exclaimed, laughing and he shrugged. "I haven't opened my other presents."

Returning to the sofa, she picked up another box and opened it to find a pair of black pumps. She looked at him quizzically. "How'd you know what size to get?"

"Do I have the right size?"

She studied the pump. "Yes, you do."

"My special magic."

"Yeah, right," she said, eyeing him and wondering when he had peeked at her things. "Well, they're perfect. Now, what's this?" She opened a fancy small box tied in a pink bow.

She opened the tiny box and lifted out a shimmering gold

racelet. "David, it's beautiful! You shouldn't have done all his."

"I wanted to," he said, taking the bracelet from her in his arge fingers. "Hold out your arm."

She did as she was told and he fastened the bracelet on her wrist. It caught glints of light from the fire as she twisted her wrist back and forth. "It's beautiful!" She looked up at him. "Thank you for everything," she said, deciding she would top arguing with him about keeping his gifts.

"Wear it all Saturday night. That's what I bought it for."

"If you have seduction in mind, I can tell you now—"

Once again he stopped her, placing his hand on her lips. "Shh, Rissa. Just wear them and look pretty. That's all. There vill be time later for seduction."

She didn't know whether to be angry or pleased, and his vords spun in her mind and she knew she would remember his moment forever. "The presents are a delight," she said, urning the bracelet and watching it reflect glints of light in he gold. "Your motive might not be. You're very sure of ourself."

"Would you rather I bite my nails when I ask you to go ut with me?"

"It would be a change."

"I'll try to be on my best behavior."

She shook her hair away from her face, crossed her legs eneath her on the sofa and turned to face him. "Thanks, gain. That was a delightful surprise."

The phone rang and David crossed the room to pick it up. He talked softly and Marissa's thoughts were on the gifts he ad given her and the coming Saturday night date.

When he replaced the receiver and sat down, his expression vas solemn. "That was Clint Andover. A man tried to slip nto our Jane Doe's room tonight."

Six

"To harm her?" Marissa asked, chilled by David's news.

"Probably, otherwise why try to sneak in?"

"Did he get away?"

"Yes. Clint had to see about our mystery Jane Doe and the intruder got a head start on Clint." David raked his finger through his hair and frowned while he thought about someone attempting to get to Autumn's mother.

"That's dreadful!"

"Someone is after her and now he knows she's in Royal. He's getting brazen about going after her. But then, for the money she was carrying, a lot of people would be willing to go to drastic lengths to get the money back."

"Do the police know?"

"Yes, they're at the hospital now, but my friend Clint will stay to guard our mystery Jane Doe." David shifted slightly closer to Marissa. "I'll need to go to town tomorrow to meet with my friends."

"David, I'd like to go see this woman and take Autumn."

"The mother's in a coma. She'd never know her baby is there," David pointed out.

"I know she's unconscious, but maybe deep down in some depths of her mind or heart, having Autumn there might make a difference. Will you ask if we can do this?"

"She has a nurse, Tara Roberts, who's taken an interest in her. We can ask Tara," he decided. "But it seems like an exercise in futility."

"I know Tara," Marissa stated. "My niece and nephews were born at Royal Memorial, so I'm familiar with some of the people there. Tara's great, and I'm glad that she's interested in this Jane Doe. Can you please find out when Tara Roberts is on duty?"

"Jane Doe's in ICU. She can't have visitors," David cautioned.

"She can have family for brief visits," she told him confidently. "And Autumn is family, more than Tara or your friend Clint who guards her."

He stared at Marissa while he appeared to mull it over. "It may not work out, but if you want to try, I'll ask. I'll go along with you, though."

"That's fine. Thanks. I'll feel better about it if mother and baby are united briefly."

"You're hopelessly optimistic," he said lightly, and she smiled.

"That's what my sister Greta always says. According to her, I'm the optimist, she's the pessimist, Karen is the party girl and Dallas is boy-crazy."

"Do you concur with the analysis?"

"Sort of," she said, smiling again.

"When I met you in the baby store and introduced myself, you said you knew me through your older sister. You look a lot younger than your sister."

"I'm twenty-eight. I often went with her to football games and I watched you play ball."

"And you remembered me from that?" he asked, and she

knew her cheeks were hot and she knew he was going to persist with his questions until he found out the answer.

"Yes, David, I remembered you. I thought you were cute. It was a schoolgirl crush. Satisfied? I got over it."

"I hope not," he said, leaning forward. "And whatever it is between us, I feel it, too."

"I suspect what *you* feel is lust."

"Damn straight. My pulse is racing right now. How about yours?" He placed his hand against her throat and waited.

She twisted away slightly. "I can't help it if my body responds to you, but that doesn't change my mind," she said, taking his hand and removing it from her throat where he had been checking her pulse. "Now, you scoot back where you were."

He grinned and scooted away a few inches, increasing the distance between them only slightly. "So tell me more about your life. How come you were working in the baby store?"

"I majored in sociology in college and that's what my degree is in. I had a job with the clinic, and after doing that for a few years, I knew I didn't want to do it forever. I have a minor in public relations and I've got applications out right now, so the store job is temporary. So where did you go to college?"

David talked about college and life on the ranch, safe topics that didn't dredge up emotions or bad memories, yet gave her a glimpse of his life. When Autumn began to cry, Marissa brought the baby to the kitchen and she and David took turns caring for her. As Marissa held and rocked her, they talked. Later that night Autumn had a second bottle, but this time when Marissa got Autumn back to sleep, she stood.

"It's almost two in the morning, David. I'm going to bed."

"Want me to carry Autumn?" he offered, standing and crossing the room to Marissa.

"No need. She's a featherweight," Marissa replied.

"I'll bring your things, then," he said, picking up the boxes of gifts he had brought her. As they left the room, he switched off the kitchen light.

"So when will we go to town tomorrow?" she asked.

"My meeting is at ten in the morning. After that, I'll talk to Clint and Tara about taking Autumn to the hospital. I don't want you wandering around alone with her. I'd rather drive back here in the afternoon and pick you two up and take you into town then."

When they reached her bedroom, he followed her inside and placed her presents on the bed. She crossed to him and caught his hand in hers. As his brows arched in surprise, she said, "Come here, David."

He went with her and she led him into the hall, pausing at the door. "Thanks for the interesting evening and dinner. Good night."

He looked amused. "You don't want me in your bedroom?"

"Not yet," she answered, and his chest expanded as he inhaled a deep breath.

"That wasn't the answer I expected, since you tricked me to get me out of your room."

Marissa smiled. "What was it you said? Sneaky and underhanded sometimes gets you what you want, or some such. Good night," she repeated with emphasis, glancing toward his bedroom.

He braced one hand against the doorjamb, blocking her way. "Just one kiss."

"You've had a kiss, and I have a baby in my arms."

"Neither matters," he said, catching her chin in his other hand and leaning down. Before he could touch her lips, Marissa ducked under his arm and stepped quickly into her bedroom.

"See you in the morning." She closed the door in his face and let out her breath. How she ached for his kisses! Every inch of her wanted to be standing outside her door in his arms. Thank heavens she had shown some restraint. Now, if she could just hang on to that restraint throughout this job.

She put Autumn in her crib, standing over the baby. Autumn was one of the most beautiful babies she had ever seen. She touched Autumn's cheek lightly with her finger. Marissa closed her eyes and said a prayer that Autumn's mother would have a full recovery. When she opened her eyes, she smoothed the baby's wispy hair. How it was going to hurt to say good-bye to Autumn!

That was one more thing she could postpone thinking about. Better to go home crying over the loss of Autumn, than to go home brokenhearted, crying over the losses of both Autumn and David. Just keep remembering that one, she told herself.

"This is no big deal. Relax and enjoy yourself." His words haunted her. It was no big deal to *him*. To her, it was enormous. The dream of half a lifetime. His sexy appeal was irresistible now. If she let the man seduce her, she would be absolute and hopeless mush around him all the time.

"Marissa Wilder, learn now to say no," she ordered aloud, remembering her ex and how charming he had been at the first. "No, no and no."

Repeating no, no, no to herself, she crossed the room to open the boxes and look again at the beautiful dress he had given her. She peeled off her T-shirt and jeans and stepped into the dress, pulling it on and sliding up the zipper, turning to look at herself in the mirror. The dress was perfection. Simple, sleek lines, short, figure-hugging, soft. She unzipped it and changed into the oversize T-shirt she slept in.

In the dark, she lay in bed and remembered David's hands on her, his touches, his fabulous kisses. Tingling, she ached and wondered whether he was really losing sleep over her or if it was just a line he used when it suited him.

She thought about the danger to the mother and to Autumn. By insisting on going to the hospital, would she put Autumn at risk? She hoped not, but she felt certain that, even though the mother wasn't conscious, she should have her baby near her for a few minutes.

Before dawn the next morning, David left the house to take care of ranch chores. He wanted to see about two of the horses and he needed to talk to his foreman.

He hadn't slept more than a couple of hours and those few hours had been fitful, waking and falling asleep again, having erotic dreams about Marissa. He suspected that she had no idea of her effect on him—that she had him tied in knots. He was looking forward eagerly to Saturday night.

He realized he better get his mind back to the possible danger they might face when they left his ranch. The attempt to get the mother was sobering. He would see Clint later today when they met at the club and he would get the details. Someone wanted that money badly. Or maybe wanted her. Or wanted to silence her. He hadn't wanted to alarm Marissa, but it seemed someone was in Royal, intent on harming their Jane Doe. None of their questions about her had been answered yet, and more had been raised.

David's thoughts jumped back to holding Marissa in his arms. Never had a woman's kisses stirred him the way hers had. He wanted so much more than kisses. He wanted her in his bed. And if she ever agreed, she knew he wasn't into lasting commitments. Just thinking about her responses to him drove his temperature skyrocketing, even in the chilly November morning. Saturday night. He groaned, knowing he had to get his thoughts elsewhere.

He wouldn't be fit for any kind of ranch work in the morning. Think about horses, he told himself. Little baby Autumn had set his life spinning like a tumbleweed in a high wind and he didn't see any chance of changing that anytime soon.

Two hours later he returned to the house to eat breakfast, shower and shave to go into town. When he headed through the house, Marissa was rocking Autumn while Gertie bustled nearby, getting things ready for supper that night. Marissa wore a dark brown sweater that clung to her figure. She had on hip-hugging jeans, and he wished Gertie was a million miles away so he could be alone with Marissa. Autumn already had her eyes closed and would soon be asleep.

"I'll call you after our meeting and let you know whether we can visit the mother today or not," he said, standing across the room from Marissa and realizing that he enjoyed watching her with Autumn. Someday she would be a great mother, he reflected. It was a notion that made him remember her intention to go to a sperm bank, which he did not want her to do. How many times was he going to have to tell himself that it was none of his business?

He left, knowing if he gave Marissa even the most casual kiss, Gertie would have word spread all over the ranch and town and Marissa would be in an uproar over the gossip.

At ten he walked through the deserted Texas Cattleman's Club to a private room to join his friends. A fire burned low in the fireplace and the coziness of the room was a contrast to the grim reason they were gathered together.

"Now we're all here," Clint said, leaning back in a large leather chair. "Howdy, David."

"How's Daddy?" Alex asked, his green eyes flashing.

"I'm fine now that I've hired Marissa Wilder."

"I'll bet you are," Ryan said. "I know Marissa. She's quite a good-looking woman."

"If she's half the party animal her sister is, you should be having a good time out there at the ranch," Alex added.

"Marissa's not a party animal. She's reliable and practical. I'm having a good time watching her take care of little Autumn. The baby is a sweetie just like Justin said, and Marissa knows babies and I can relax and enjoy my life once again."

"You didn't have to take care of that tiny baby single-handedly for even twenty-four hours and you sound like you were overworked for a month," Alex teased.

"Can it, Alex. I'm thankful to have a competent nanny. Haven't even noticed her looks."

Ryan whistled. "Either he's lying or someone needs to take his temperature because he's the walking dead," he joked, and David grinned.

"All right, we're all here," David said. "Let's hear what happened, Clint." David sat on another leather chair, his friends already seated around the room.

"I caught him by the bed," Clint said, his long legs stretched in front of him. In a black sweater he looked dark, brooding and formidable. David thought the intruder was desperate to try to sneak past someone as dangerous-looking as Clint.

"It looked like to me that the guy was starting to pick her up," Clint said. "I don't know whether he meant to hurt her or if he intended to kidnap her. He had already looked in her locker because her few possessions were in disarray. I tried to grab him, but in the scuffle, he broke loose. It was a choice of chasing him or seeing to Jane Doe. I stopped to see if she was all right. She had top priority," he said, and the others murmured agreement.

"I yelled for help," Clint continued, "so nurses arrived in a hurry. As soon as they were in the room, I went after the guy, but he'd had a head start and got clean away," Clint finished grimly.

"You can't identify him?" Ryan asked, his brown-eyed gaze on Clint.

"No. He was tall enough—around six feet, not heavy, plenty muscular, I could tell that when we struggled for a moment. He had a ski mask pulled over his face so I didn't get hair color or features before he ran away."

"Did you ever see him in the light? Even at a distance?" David asked.

Raking his dark brown hair away from his forehead, Clint shook his head. "The only time I glimpsed him in the light was when he was running down a hallway. His back was to me and he wore jeans, a denim jacket and a black ski mask. How generic is that? He had on sneakers. There was nothing distinguishing. All I got was his approximate height, not too heavy, and he was damned strong."

"Did he get in a car?" Ryan asked, and Clint shook his head.

"He doubled back and I think he went into the hospital again. There are entrances all over that old hospital. It's been modernized and built onto. I hate to say it, but, guys, I lost him."

"Nobody's blaming you," David said quickly. "You think he went back inside the hospital?"

"Who knows? I told the police about him, and they searched the building and grounds for hours. Some of them are probably still searching. They have guards stationed at various places and one took over for me so I could leave for a time."

"Do you think the guy was armed?" Alex asked.

"If he was, I didn't see the weapon," Clint replied. "I don't know what he was trying to do with her."

"Either way, she's in danger, as we suspected," David remarked, thinking about Autumn, Marissa and Gertie at his ranch house. Was it as safe as he had led Marissa to believe? he wondered. He shifted in his chair. "Alex, any leads? Have you found out anything else?"

Alex shook his head. "I haven't turned up one clue. The police haven't, either. No one seems to be legitimately searching for her. No woman and baby with their description are on any missing persons lists the sheriff has."

"What about that list of names that was in the bag she carried?"

"I'm working on it, but I can't find a trace of them."

David nodded. "I've warned Marissa, Gertie and the guys who work for me. Dad's out of the country and I see no reason to contact him over this."

"Naw, your dad isn't mixed in this, I'm sure. But you are," Clint remarked grimly.

"Same goes for you. You're really in his way."

"I'd just like to get my hands on him."

"All of us would," David said. "I wonder if he's the father."

"Seems as if he would come forward if he were the father. With the kind of money she was carrying, who knows what she's tangled up in."

"She was terrified that night," David said, still remembering looking down into her eyes. "Beneath the bruises and starvation, she was young and attractive. Showgirl? Model? We have no idea what we're dealing with here."

"I know," Clint said, standing. "I better go. We'll just continue as we were and hope we get a break."

Leaving the club, they split up, except David fell into step beside Clint. "I need to get some groceries, go home and then take Marissa to the hospital if it's all right," David said as they crossed the parking lot.

"I'll call you, but I feel certain Tara will agree about bringing the baby to the hospital."

"Thanks, Clint. Stop worrying. You may get another chance at the guy."

"I don't want our Jane Doe hurt, but I hope I do get another round with him," Clint told him. "I won't be taken by surprise again."

"You have my cell number. I'll wait for your call."

"Sure thing. Thanks for the positive thoughts, David."

"You're welcome," David said as the two men parted. David headed for his sports car in quick, long strides, anxious to get back to the ranch. Marissa could be in danger, and he hated that he had put her in such danger by hiring her.

Before he started the engine, David called Rusty, his foreman, and warned him, asking him to have someone keep an eye on the house.

As soon as he replaced the receiver, David started the engine and drove to the store, hurrying to make his purchases and then heading back to the ranch, knowing he was above the speed limit, yet feeling an urgency to get to Marissa and Autumn. Now, more than ever, he hated to bring the two of them into Royal, but he had promised and he would stay right beside her. He had been in situations a hundred times more risky than this one and not worried, so he wondered why he was uptight now?

Before he reached the ranch, he received a call from Clint that Tara had said it was okay to bring Marissa and Autumn to the hospital to see their Jane Doe.

It was four in the afternoon when he drove back into Royal

with his two passengers. Seated in the car beside him, Marissa wore a black jacket over her brown sweater and jeans. The chilly air had put more pink in her cheeks, and as he drove, David was intensely aware that it had been hours since he had kissed her or been alone with her. She looked fantastic and she was bubbly, delighted to go to the hospital and excited about taking Autumn for an outing even though the baby didn't know or care.

He hadn't said anything else to Marissa about the danger because he intended to protect them and he didn't see a need to worry her.

When he had returned to the ranch earlier, Marissa had surprised him. Since they would be in Royal, anyway, she had asked him if he would like to have dinner at her grandmother's house so he could meet the part of her family that was living in Royal.

He agreed, but now he wished he could postpone the meeting and get Marissa back to the ranch and to himself. He knew he couldn't and he knew he should meet her family. He could understand why they were curious about him since Marissa had moved to his ranch, but he still wished he could have her all to himself.

At the hospital, he kept his arm around Marissa's waist while she carried little Autumn. The baby was asleep, unaware of what was going on around her. She was dressed in a pink bunting and looked adorable. David was surprised how much he was beginning to care for the child and he could understand Justin's statement that after three days with her, he wouldn't ever want to give her up.

On the other hand, he wasn't ready for marriage, commitment or babies in his life on a permanent basis. He glanced down at Marissa and inhaled deeply, remembering again her remarks about going to a sperm bank. She wanted a saint. Well, no hope there for him, but what she said and what she *did* were worlds apart.

He watched people around them, particularly men, although he knew there could be more than one person after Jane Doe.

On the Intensive Care Unit floor, David asked for Tara Roberts and was told to have a seat in the waiting room. David took Marissa's arm to head across the hall to the waiting room, which had only two other people in it. Glancing at the sleeping baby, David wondered how long Autumn would sleep, because she had slept all the ride into Royal from his ranch.

"Mr. Sorrenson?" A tall, shapely blonde with friendly green eyes crossed to them and smiled at Marissa. "Hi, Marissa."

"Hi, Tara," Marissa answered easily as she and David stood.

"Is this our Jane Doe's little girl?" Tara asked, a soft note entering her voice.

"Thank you for arranging to get mother and baby together," Marissa said. "Common sense says it won't make any difference, but my heart tells me differently."

"It won't hurt," Tara said firmly. "Just have a seat a few more minutes and I'll come and get you. Only Marissa and the baby can go into the room, Mr. Sorrenson."

"Tara, just call me David. That's fine."

She left and in minutes returned to get them. David trailed along to greet Clint and wait with his friend while Marissa went with Tara.

"Just a few minutes and then you'll have to leave," Tara instructed, and led Marissa into a small room filled with hospital equipment.

The only sounds were the hiss and beep of equipment. Marissa drew a deep breath, feeling a great sadness at the sight of Autumn's mother, hooked up to machines, lying so still in the bed. The woman was pale and looked painfully fragile and small.

"Tara, can I place the baby in the bed with her?" Marissa whispered.

"Let me do it," Tara replied quietly, and took Autumn to lay her on top of the covers at the mother's side. "Here's your little girl. Your baby," Tara said softly.

Feeling a tightness in her throat, Marissa sat in the chair, watching, knowing it was just as David had said, an exercise in futility, yet still feeling that the mother-child bond might reach down into some dark depth that nothing else could. If it were her in place of Jane Doe, she would want someone to put her baby close beside her. Marissa closed her eyes to pray because Autumn needed her mother. And her mother needed Autumn. If her only words before losing consciousness had been about her baby, she had to care that her baby was safe.

Tara moved away from the bed to stand on the other side of the room, and Marissa sat quietly, watching Autumn and Jane Doe. The only indication that the woman was alive was the rise and fall of her chest as she breathed.

Then Autumn stirred, opening her eyes and beginning to fuss, and in a second she started to cry. Tara stepped up to the bed to pick her up.

"It's probably been long enough," the nurse said reluctantly. "Though the crying won't disturb the mother."

"I hope she recovers," Marissa said, taking Autumn in her arms and holding the baby close. At the door she turned to look again at the unknown woman who looked so frail and pale. "Get well," she whispered. "Your baby needs you."

Autumn's cries escalated and Marissa wanted to cry with her as she held the baby close, cuddling her and telling herself that Autumn's cries were because of hunger, nothing else. Autumn couldn't know about her mother, but to Marissa, in spite of logic, it still seemed like Autumn was crying for her mother.

She met David's gaze and saw he was watching her intently. He stood with a tall, solemn brown-haired man whose attention was on Tara.

"Marissa, this is Clint Andover," David said, "my friend who is keeping watch over Jane Doe."

As Clint said hello, he stepped closer to look at Autumn. "How's the little one?"

"She's fine. Hungry right now," Marissa replied, holding Autumn against her shoulder while she patted her back.

"Thanks again, Tara," Marissa said to the nurse while David thanked her, also. David took Marissa's arm and they walked away while Tara turned to talk to Clint.

"She's a good nurse," Marissa said. "She really cares."

"I'm glad. And Clint is one tough guard. Even though a guy slipped past him, Clint prevented anything bad from happening to her. I'm sure our Jane Doe will be safe."

"I'll ride in back so Autumn can be buckled into her seat and I can feed her," Marissa said. "She's stopped crying, but I know she's hungry."

"Just feed her here," David said, opening the car door for Marissa. "We'll wait until you're through. It won't take long."

She nodded and got out a bottle and settled in the passenger seat to hold Autumn close and give her a bottle. As Autumn drank, Marissa said, "Thanks for setting up that hospital visit. I know you think it was a bunch of foolishness."

He smiled. "As you said, who knows what will come of it. It didn't hurt, and if it helped, then that's good. You're a compassionate person, Marissa Wilder," he said.

She smiled in return, but she remembered Reed, who often told her she was a good person. Good, practical, helpful, but not the kind to inspire truly deep passion. David was passionate about her, but she was a convenience, under his roof and available when he had nothing else to do. Now she wondered if he was constantly around more to guard Autumn than because he wanted to be in her presence.

She looked outside at wind tossing leaves in the parking lot. David felt lust, no doubt about that, but she suspected that was all it was. She knew she was vulnerable, uncertain of herself in some ways because of the hurtful things her ex-husband had said. He had accused her of not being passionate, not being enough of a woman for him. She sighed and tried to shut all of the past out of her thoughts, turning to look at Autumn, who was once again asleep.

"Ready?" David asked.

She nodded and gave him directions to her grandmother's house in an older area of Royal. They parked in front of a redbrick, two-story house with neat flower beds surrounding the front. As they went up the front walk, Marissa took David's arm. "Grandma doesn't believe in the dangers of cholesterol. I think she told me she would fry chicken tonight."

"Sounds good to me."

Pots of greenery flanked the front door. Marissa pushed the doorbell and then reached to open the door, but before she could, it flew out of her hand.

When the door swung open, David gazed at a short grayhaired woman dressed in a blue sweater and gray slacks. Her enormous brown eyes were as piercing and alert as her granddaughter's and David had a peculiar feeling that this visit was not a casual "meet my family" time as much as an opportunity for Marissa's granny to check him out.

"This is my grandmother, Louise Wilder," Marissa said. "Grandma, meet David Sorrenson."

"How do you do, Mrs. Wilder?" he said politely, holding Autumn with one hand while he shook Louise Wilder's thin hand.

"Howdy-do, Mr. Sorrenson. Let me see that precious little baby," she said, taking the baby from David. He wondered if he had been totally dismissed from her attention. As she turned away with Autumn, Marissa took his arm and they stepped inside an entryway to meet two young women who bore a resemblance to Marissa.

"This is my sister Greta," Marissa said, and David greeted a slender brunette, taller than Marissa with large brown eyes and a winning smile. She didn't look younger than Marissa, but he knew she was. Then he turned as Marissa introduced her youngest sister. "And this is Dallas."

He greeted another pretty girl, who had her long brown hair caught behind her head in a red bow that matched her red T-shirt. She giggled and grinned and gave him a lingering handshake.

"Let's go join Grandma," Marissa suggested, and David was aware of her hand on his arm. Tempting smells of baking bread, frying chicken and the inviting aroma of hot cider as-

sailed him as Marissa led him into a large family room, where
Grandma Wilder was already seated in a large rocking chair.
She rocked and talked softly to Autumn. The baby's eyes were
open and she seemed content to be in Louise Wilder's arms.

"Your whole family must have the magic touch with
babies," David commented. As they talked, David decided his
hunch was correct about why he had been invited to dinner.
While Louise Wilder gave plenty of attention to Autumn, she
asked him specific questions about his life and background.
They chatted, and soon Marissa's sisters excused themselves
and disappeared into the kitchen to get dinner on the table.

During dinner, Grandma Wilder learned that David played
chess and Marissa laughed. "Grandma, don't make David play
chess with you. Grandma is a chess nut and likes to play
whenever she gets the chance."

"It's fine with me," David replied politely, knowing he
couldn't eat and run, but wanting to get Marissa home.

After dinner, Marissa, Dallas and Greta insisted on cleaning
the dishes and shooed him off to the chess match. All of the
Wilder women took turns with Autumn, who seemed blissfully
happy in their care.

And David found Louise Wilder to be a formidable oppo-
nent. Within minutes, he had to concentrate on chess, because
he realized he was playing with an expert. He did all right
until Marissa finished with the kitchen cleaning and came to
sit near him. He watched her walk across the room with that
sexy sway of her hips that fascinated him. The brown sweater
clung and defined her full breasts and tiny waist, and he had
a fleeting vision of peeling her out of it later in the evening
when they were alone. She pulled a chair close beside him to
watch, flashing one of her winning, dimpled smiles at him.

With Marissa only inches from him, his concentration on
chess shattered, and it took an effort to salvage the damage of
several bad moves. Dallas pulled up a chair close on the other
side of him, trying to flirt with him until Greta called her away.

He was aware of passing time, of Marissa watching, sitting
close enough he could detect her perfume. Occasionally she

would comment, but most of the time she was quiet while Greta and Dallas took turns with Autumn or let Grandma Wilder hold the baby when she wanted to.

When he had started, he'd intended to *let* Louise Wilder win, but now he knew she would win no matter how he played. He wanted to get back to the ranch with Marissa, yet he didn't feel he had a good excuse to cut the game short.

"You're very good," Grandma Wilder remarked at one point, and he looked into sharp brown eyes, wondering if she approved or disapproved of him. And he wondered at himself and why he really cared whether he had her approval or not. After tonight he didn't imagine he would ever see her again.

"I think it's getting late and I give way to a champion," he said when he noticed the tall clock across the room showed ten minutes after eleven. "You win," he conceded.

"Well, we haven't finished, so who knows?" the old woman replied with a wink, and smiled at him. She still held Autumn, who was sleeping peacefully.

"I'll make hot chocolate before you leave," Greta said, and was off to the kitchen.

"Don't go to the trouble. We should go—"

"We can stay for a cup of hot chocolate," Marissa broke in, smiling at him. "All right?"

Looking at her smile, he knew he would have agreed to most anything she wanted and he nodded. In minutes, they were all seated around the oval oak kitchen table with steaming mugs of hot chocolate and a platter of Louise Wilder's cookies. Autumn had wakened, and Grandma Wilder was giving the infant her bottle.

"You said your father is out of the country, David," Marissa said. "If he isn't here for Thanksgiving, why don't you come and eat with us? Or if he is here, invite him, too."

This was seconded by the girls and Grandma Wilder.

"Thanks, that's kind of you to invite me," David said. But he wasn't expecting to have Marissa around by Thanksgiving. And if she moved out, would they date? He knew he wanted to, but he thought how persuasive he had to be to get her out with him Saturday night. At least now he had a date with her for Thanksgiving, even if it was with her whole family.

It was half past midnight before they were finally in the car headed to the ranch. Driving through the cold, dark night, he was anxious to get home. His pulse was drumming, because when they got to his house, he could finally be alone with Marissa.

As they walked into the house, Autumn woke. David helped Marissa get a bottle, turned the lights low, built a fire and then sat and watched while Marissa fed Autumn and rocked her back to sleep. David stood as soon as Autumn was soundly asleep. "I'll put her in bed for you and then we can talk."

Marissa stood and smiled at him. "I'll take her to bed. It's late, David, and I'm exhausted. I'll tell you good night now and see you in the morning."

Disappointment and frustration rocked him. "Aw, Marissa, just a little while. Tomorrow when morning comes, I'll take care of Autumn and you can sleep in."

Shaking her head, Marissa walked away. "It's very late. I'll see you in the morning."

He hurried to catch up with her in the hallway, walking to her bedroom door where she turned to hand him an empty bottle. "I forgot to leave this in the kitchen. Do you mind?"

"Sure," he said, taking the bottle and starting to reach for her. She stepped into her room, half closing the door and smiling at him again.

"See you in the morning." She closed the door and was gone.

He stared at the door, tempted to simply open it and step inside and kiss away her protests because he knew he could. On the other hand, she had made it clear what she wanted, and he wasn't accustomed to pushing himself when a woman didn't want him around.

He realized he was still rooted in front of her door as minutes ticked by. Swearing under his breath, he turned and went to his room, feeling more hot and bothered than ever.

* * *

Saturday morning David was caught up in ranch chores and in the afternoon Gertie was around, something he couldn't remember happening before on Saturday afternoons.

He discovered that she was helping Marissa with some baking and the house was filled with tempting smells, but his appetite had fled. He was counting the minutes until their night out, whereas, if Marissa was filled with anticipation, she hid it totally.

Marissa bathed Autumn and dressed her in white fleece pajamas for the evening, packing the girl's little bag with everything she might need. Marissa had closed the door to her room, wanting privacy, trying to keep some distance from David, because her reaction to the sexy Texan was too intense.

Even though she took her time bathing and washing her hair, blowing her hair dry, getting dressed, happiness bubbled in her. All day she had tried to avoid thinking about tonight, but had failed completely because it was constantly on her mind. She was with him twenty-four hours a day here at his house, so why did a night out with him stir her beyond measure? The thought of just the two of them was exciting; the prospect of dancing with him heightened her eagerness.

She slipped into a black lace bra and panties, pulled on panty hose and then the dress, which was lined with silk, making it cool against her skin.

Combing her hair, she twisted and pinned it up on her head and put on small, gold hoop earrings and the gold bracelet David had given her. Finally she looked at herself in her mirror, pleased with her reflection, thinking the dress was one of the most beautiful dresses she had ever owned.

As she studied her reflection, she reminded herself of her disastrous marriage. She didn't want to make the same mistake a second time—yet there would be no marriage where David was involved. He had made that abundantly clear. Forever, she would remember his words. *This is no big deal so you relax and enjoy yourself.*

"Be careful tonight," she whispered to her image, wondering if all caution was useless.

She picked up a small black bag, looked at Autumn, who was asleep in her crib, and had a pang about leaving her for a few hours. Shaking her head, Marissa knew that someday soon she was going to have to leave Autumn forever. That hurt, yet more than anything else, Marissa wanted the little baby back with her mother. With a sigh, Marissa left to find David.

Waiting until they were ready to go out the door to get Autumn to take her to the Windovers', Marissa saw no point in disturbing the baby until they had to.

She found him in the family room, looking breathtakingly handsome in his navy suit. He stood by one of the windows, gazing outside at the dusky evening. "I'm ready, David," she said.

Seven

David's appearance was entirely too sexy and dangerous for her peace of mind. His gaze drifted over her and then he looked into her eyes and she inhaled deeply.

"You're gorgeous," he said in a thick voice.

"You are, too," she whispered, trying to catch her breath.

He slipped his arms around her waist and his smoldering gaze traveled slowly over her features. "I'd like to take down your hair and peel you out of that dress."

"Instead, you're taking me out to dinner and dancing," she replied, trying to sound firm, hoping he couldn't hear her pounding heart.

"I've been looking forward to this all day," she admitted.

"You hid it well. I couldn't tell if you were interested in our date or not, but I'm glad to hear that you were."

"I've been looking forward to this for eons, David," she said, and his eyes darkened.

"If you say a few more things like that to me, we might not leave the house."

"Then I'll be very careful what I say. Very impersonal things, like it's a cold night and we have to wake Autumn before we go."

David caressed her throat with warm, feathery touches that were devastating. "Sure you don't want to stay here and go out tomorrow night instead?" he asked in a hushed and velvety tone.

"I'm absolutely positive. Don't try to wriggle out of the date you promised me."

He smiled and trailed his fingers along her cheek. "I won't wriggle out of any date with you. Shall we get the baby and go?"

"Fine," she replied. As they walked through the house to the bedroom, Marissa said, "I talked to Grandma today. You were a hit with my family and Grandma was impressed with your chess playing. Needless to say, my sister Dallas was gaga over your looks, but don't let that go to your head because Dallas is fascinated with any and all good-looking males."

"Well, I'm glad I'm liked, but there is only one Wilder I'm really concerned about impressing."

"You don't have to be concerned. I've been impressed since I was eleven years old."

He caught her around the waist and swung her around to face him, holding her in a light embrace. "When you say things like that, how do you expect me to react any way except physically?"

"You've had a lot of experience with women, David. You can take flirty remarks like mine coolly because, I imagine, you've had a spectacular effect on females all your life."

"Well, damn few of them have told me so. It's different coming from you. Every statement from you about how appealing you find me just makes me want to do something about it."

She laughed. "What you *can* do about it is take me dining and dancing."

To her surprise he scowled. "You think that's funny, but you're setting me on fire here. I'll get my revenge tonight.

Sweet revenge,'' he said in a voice that ran across her nerves, and she knew she was flirting with danger, especially if she wanted him to slow down and keep his distance.

"All right. I'll be very circumspect."

"The hell with that. I can tell you now that I have no intention of being circumspect."

"Down, fella," she told him. "I've been looking forward to this, and I'm excited about getting to see the Texas Cattleman's Club that is such a male bastion and *the* club in these parts."

"We do let females in for parties," David told her, still gazing at her.

"Let's see about Autumn." Marissa walked away from him toward the baby's room. She glanced over her shoulder to find him still watching her intently.

She went to get the baby carrier and bundled Autumn into it. "Everything is packed except the bottles of formula," she told David when she rejoined him.

"I have them ready and waiting in the kitchen. I'll take Autumn," David replied as he crossed the room to kneel beside the baby carrier. Marissa stood beside it, and David reached across the few inches that separated them and ran his fingers lightly along her leg, up beneath her skirt a few inches until she stepped away.

"David!" Marissa gasped, trying to steady herself on her feet.

"Just a feel before we go. Anticipation, darlin'," he drawled in a honeyed voice, making her heart skip.

As he picked up the carrier, she grabbed the diaper bag, hurrying to the kitchen to pack the bottles.

"Where's your coat?" he asked, glancing around the kitchen.

"I'm not wearing one. You'll keep me warm."

His smoldering green gaze met hers. "There you go again. You better believe me, I'll keep you warm. Come here."

"I'm fine right now."

"It's cold out there."

"I'll run," she said, laughing at his attempts to get her close.

He turned on the alarms and switched off the lights. Just as she was going out the back door, he pulled her against him. "I said that I'll keep you warm," he said, putting his arm around her shoulders. They rushed through a cold, clear evening, the last faint rays of sunshine still making their surroundings dusky and visible.

He started the engine and the heater, held the door for Marissa, and then buckled Autumn into the back. Finally, he slid behind the wheel and they left, speeding through the night to another area ranch that belonged to Jason and Meredith Windover.

As the car stopped near the door of the ranch house, it opened and a couple stepped outside. David introduced Marissa to his tall, black-haired friend Jason, who was another handsome Texan. She met Meredith Windover, short, redheaded, whose warm, welcoming smile made Marissa feel she had known Meredith a long time.

They carried sleeping Autumn inside and peeked at Ian Windover, who was asleep in his crib, his head covered in thick black ringlets.

"Thank you for keeping her," Marissa said.

"Don't worry. Just have a good time. We're experienced at this by now," Meredith reassured her.

"We'll keep her tonight and tomorrow if you want a break," Jason offered. "Two babies should be a hoot."

"Two babies would be chaos," David said, grinning. "Nope, but thanks. We'll pick her up tonight and I'll call you when we head back to the ranch."

"We won't stay out late, I promise," Marissa added, feeling pangs again about leaving Autumn.

"We stay up late on Saturday nights," Jason replied. "Take your time and don't worry. We have your cell phone number and can get in touch with you should any need arise."

They told the Windovers goodbye and soon were back in the car, headed to the highway to Royal.

Twisting in the seat to look back at the ranch house, which had lights illuminating the yard and the outbuildings surrounding it, Marissa shivered.

"What's wrong?" David asked, reaching over to take her hand in his, placing their hands on his warm thigh.

She inhaled, electricity streaking up her arm and spreading through her from the physical contact with him. "Even if your friends are very good parents, I feel a little uneasy, leaving her there. And now that I know there's a chance she might be in some danger, I can't help thinking about how isolated these ranch houses are."

"They're fortresses. Jason Windover and I have both had training that covers all kinds of dangerous situations. There are lots of people on these ranches, tough cowboys who aren't afraid to come to the rescue or wade into a fight. We all have alarms, dogs, lights. Autumn will be safe tonight. I promise you. Stop worrying."

She tried to smile at him, but her thoughts were still back on the baby.

David released her hand, placing his hand on her knee and sliding his fingers up along her thigh while he drove with his other hand.

Erotic sensations heated her, and she caught his wrist, pulling his hand out from beneath her skirt. "David," she warned.

"Just wanted to take your mind off worrying over Autumn," he answered lightly. "I think I succeeded."

"You succeeded beyond your wildest imaginings!" she snapped, her breasts tingling and heat charging her.

"That's one of the things I like about you," he said quietly. "You say what you're thinking. It makes life interesting."

"You better get your mind on driving. We're reaching the highway."

"I can drive and talk about you at the same time."

"You don't know me well enough to talk about me very much."

"I'm getting to know you and I already have learned a lot. You say what you think. You react to my kisses, react to my touch. I know about your family, about your job and boss. See, I know a lot. I'll know a lot more after tonight. I want to know how you feel and taste, every inch of you,'' he said in a mellow, intimate tone that was seductive.

"Dream on, fella. You're into short relationships,'' she said, exhilaration bubbling in her that she tried to ignore. "I'm not. Get that through your handsome head.''

"Half of what you say is yes and half of what you say is no,'' he said quietly, running his thumb over her knuckles again, holding her hand on his thigh.

"Half is my heart talking and the other half is my mind, and my mind is the one in control,'' she answered, watching him and hoping she could live up to what she was saying.

"We'll see about that,'' he answered, his attention on the road while she studied his masculine profile, his jaw that indicated he was accustomed to getting what he wanted.

He slowed the car on the circular drive to the Texas Cattleman's Club's entrance and stopped under the portico to let a valet take his car. A cool breeze blew gently over Marissa when she stepped out of the car while David took her hand.

As they entered the rambling two-and-a-half-story clubhouse, she looked around, curious about every facet of the club. She was impressed with the elegance of the dark, polished walnut paneling that complemented the thick Oriental rugs and the oil paintings in ornate gilt frames.

With her arm linked through David's, Marissa entered the dining room where linen-covered tables circled a dance floor. She was aware David greeted nearly every person they saw while she knew quite a few herself.

As they were seated in a corner beside a window, Marissa's appetite fled. Giving her his undivided attention, David reached across the linen-covered table to take her hand, and it wasn't until their waiter appeared that David released her. All the time he held her hand, his thumb stroked her knuckles lightly, slowly fueling flames already ignited at the ranch and in the car.

David ordered wine and after it had been poured and they

were alone, he raised his glass slightly. "Here's to a memorable evening," he said.

She touched her glass against his with the faintest clink and watched him over the rim as she sipped. Relishing every moment, she felt giddy, dazzled by him.

They sipped their wine while they looked at menus. Marissa's attention was on David, not the menu, and she found it difficult to think about ordering or what she wanted to eat.

"Steaks and barbecue are the specialties here," he said.

"I'll have the rib eye," she said, looking at David's thick, black hair as he bent his head over the menu.

Marissa knew that in spite of all his arguments, tonight could never be taken casually, never be just a pleasant time for a few hours out together. She knew that all her life she would remember every minute of this night. From tiny details, like the rosebud in a vase on the table, to the handsome man facing her, everything was more vivid than normal, and was unforgettable. With his rugged good looks and his charm, David was intoxicating.

She had dreamed of this night too often in her life. And that was all the more reason that she should have turned him down. Once again, she had placed her heart in jeopardy.

The waiter took their orders, with David ordering a sirloin while she had the rib eye. The waiter said he would be back shortly with salads.

A couple passed the table and greeted David, smiling at her as they walked by.

"I think you must know everyone in the county."

"I know a lot of people and you probably do, too. But right now, we're in the club where I know all the members and they know me."

"David, this is a dream come true!" she exclaimed. "My first date with you, my first time in the Texas Cattleman's Club. It will be my first dance with you."

He groaned. "You make me want to yank you up out of here and go straight home."

"Never! I'm going to enjoy this evening!"

"I hope you do, Rissa," he said quietly. "I want you to really enjoy it. I want it to be special because it's already special for me."

"David," she whispered, and he reached across the table to take her hand again.

The waiter appeared, and David released her hand while green salads were placed before them. A small golden loaf of bread was placed on the table on a plank with a knife and cold pats of golden butter.

Over salad and when their entrées arrived, she and David talked about Autumn and the mystery surrounding her mother. Marissa ate slowly, far more interested in David than in eating, and she noticed he wasn't eating much, either.

She sipped the deep red wine and cut into her steak, trying to calm her quivering heart and cling to wisdom. Eat, dance a couple of dances and pick up Autumn. Go home and keep a distance from David, she told herself, eating in silence while he reached across the table to touch her cheek. "Your eyes are beautiful," he said. "Dark brown, mysterious, hiding secrets from me. Hiding what you feel, what you're thinking."

"Not hiding enough," she said. "You know I usually say what I think."

He smiled at her, creases bracketing his mouth. "That's good. Then I know what's going on in that mind of yours. I wish that schoolgirl crush had never ended."

"You know full well there are residual effects from it. I respond to you. I have an effect on you, too."

"That's the understatement of the night," he replied quietly. "Marissa, give up that sperm bank idea. That's crazy. You're beautiful, sexy— You are so many things that will attract a man. Don't go the sperm bank route. And stop searching for a saint. You won't ever find him."

"I'm not searching for him. I don't want another unhappy marriage, love affair, relationship, whatever category it falls in."

"But you want a baby."

"Oh, my, yes! When you give up Autumn, won't it hurt?"

she asked him. "Won't you want a little baby girl to fill her place?"

"It'll hurt for a brief time, but I think that will pass. No, I don't want another baby around just because I find Autumn adorable."

"You're a hardhearted man, David Sorrenson. A man who is into shallow relationships," she teased.

"And you're a softhearted woman who is into impossible relationships."

The band began to play, and David glanced at their half-eaten dinners. "Let's dance," he said, and stood, taking her hand.

Smiling up at him, she stood and went to the dance floor. They passed people who knew David, and he stopped to introduce her and chat with them. Marissa saw a few people she knew, but she was more aware of the elegant, beautiful women who spoke to David, the kind of women she thought he was far more accustomed to dating.

"I wish I had you all to myself," he said when they finally reached the dance floor three numbers later. David pulled her into his arms for a slow dance, and she inhaled deeply, catching the scent of his aftershave, feeling the soft wool of his suit jacket against her arm and hand. She wound her fingers in his thick hair at the back of his head and looked up at this man who was both marvelous and a dangerous threat to her future.

He was warm, his coat was unbuttoned, swinging open as he danced. She was drowning in green eyes that held their own seduction with the desire that blazed in their depths.

She moved with him as if they had danced together all their lives. No missteps here on the dance floor. She knew the missteps would be the mistakes her heart would make, the vulnerability she had around this man who had always appealed to her.

In minutes the music changed to a fast tune and she was dancing in front of David, who watched her and laughed. "I told you it would be exciting to get out, didn't I?" he asked as he passed her.

"Yes, yes!" she gasped, swaying in front of him. He caught her hand to spin her around and turn her back, releasing her. Fine beads of perspiration dotted his brow as they danced and she forgot caution, enjoying moving with David, watching him and knowing that he was watching her just as intently.

Between dances David shed his coat and they returned to the dance floor where he pulled her into his arms to slow dance. "This is good, holding you close, moving with you, feeling you against me. I've been dreaming of this since the first night we were together."

"I've been dreaming of this since sixth grade," she replied dryly, and smiled at him. "But don't let that go to your head because I'm older and wiser now."

"I don't know about older and wiser, but for sure, prettier and sexier."

"Phooey! You didn't know I was alive. I have been introduced to you probably a half dozen times."

"Until this last time I'll bet you weren't sixteen years old."

"Maybe not, but I was still me."

"Still adorable little Rissa," he teased. "That first morning I met you, I thought you were one strange gal—dressed up in those clothes. Not that I cared, believe me."

"I know. You were just looking for any living, breathing person who could take care of little Autumn. Your friends made a good choice giving her to you. You did your best and you were careful and conscientious. You learn fast."

"Thanks," he replied dryly.

"After Autumn goes back to her mother, are you moving to Houston to take that job?"

"Yes, but I'll wait another month or two probably," David answered, not telling her that he was thinking of sticking around Royal because of her. "There's no big rush. I just want a break between the military and going to work at the oil company," he answered.

His nonchalance made her realize they lived in different worlds. While her family was comfortable, they could never live like David.

"Once I go down there, I'm locked into it," he added. "I don't want that yet."

"If you don't want to work in Houston, why don't you just stay on the ranch?" she asked.

He shrugged one shoulder and tightened his arm around her waist, pulling her closer against him. "I've been raised to do that job. When I was in college, I used to work summers there. Dad expects it of me and I've never let him down. I don't have a good reason to refuse it."

"Just that your heart isn't in it and you don't want to. I know your father can afford to hire good people who could do the job."

"Oh, sure. He just wants this to stay in the family."

"But it can't always stay in the family."

"So what are you suggesting I should do?" he asked, looking down at her with amusement in his eyes, and she knew he wouldn't pay any attention to her suggestions.

"You said you love the ranch. Why not work there?"

He shrugged and then gazed beyond her as if looking into the distance. "I've just always known I was going to go into the oil business like Dad planned."

"How much would it disappoint him really if you didn't go to work in Houston?"

"I don't know. I never considered doing anything else," David replied, and smiled at her, his gaze going over her features. "That's in the future. Right now, I know what I want to do."

"I don't think I want to hear this one," she replied.

"I want to take down your hair," he said, bending to whisper in her ear and nuzzle her neck, "hold you close, kiss you and make you lose all this caution that you keep wrapped around you like a suit of armor."

While she quivered, his arm tightened until she was pressed against him, thigh against thigh, her breasts against his chest, his strong arms holding her as they danced and he kissed her ear.

Wisdom screamed stop, but need was hot, aching. She

wanted him beyond her wildest dreams. She wound her arms around his neck to slow dance with him, a dance of seduction. The clean, cottony smell of his shirt, his aftershave, the hard feel of him, everything about him was torment and pleasure.

"Let's go home, Rissa," he whispered. The words were magic, thrilling her, but she had been hurt deeply in the past and it was easy to see that she was hurtling toward another big crash tonight if she didn't stop.

She leaned away to look up at him, trying to get her breath and wishing her heart would cease hammering. "Since I was eleven years old I've been waiting to go dancing with you. I don't want to cut the night short now."

A faint smile tugged at one corner of his mouth. "Then we'll stay and dance, but I don't think you've been eagerly dreaming of this moment all these years."

"Maybe not, but being with you has revived all those old fantasies."

"Like what?" he asked, his brows arching.

"You're self-confident enough now without me boosting your ego one bit more. I have no intention of telling you what dreams I had that involved you."

"Want me to tell you the dreams I had last night that involved you?"

"No!" she exclaimed, feeling her cheeks heat just from the look in his eyes. She knew he was amused, but he was coming on strong and he was far too irresistible.

The next number was another fast one and David released her. Dancing in time to the thundering beat, she was enveloped in his gaze.

When the band took a break, David picked up his coat to lead her out on the terrace, where he draped the coat around her shoulders and pulled her into his arms. Golden light spilled from the windows, with black shadows in between, and the air had grown chillier, yet she wasn't aware of anything except the tall man holding her.

She put her hands against his chest and looked up at him. "It's a wonderful night. You were right. I'm having a grand time, but I'd like to call and ask about Autumn and see how things are going.''

''Worrier,'' he teased. ''I can assure you that Autumn is in good hands. Do you want to make the call or shall I?''

''If you don't mind, you go ahead. You know the Windovers better than I do.''

David fished his cell phone out of a coat pocket, punched numbers and in minutes was talking to someone. She knew from his part of the conversation that all was well, and in seconds David confirmed what she had deduced. He told Jason Windover goodbye and turned off his phone to return it to his pocket.

''Thanks,'' she said, feeling foolish but relieved to hear Autumn was fine. ''I know I worry needlessly about her, but she's so tiny and she's already had enough happen in her life.''

''That's true, Rissa.'' He leaned down to kiss her ear, his warm breath tantalizing, and then he trailed kisses to her mouth, brushing her lips lightly.

Marissa stood on tiptoe, turning her face up to his as his lips settled, possessed, and he kissed her deeply.

She returned his kiss, longing becoming a tight coil, a curling need deep inside her that made her want to step across the restrictions she had set for herself and to take what he offered and live life on his terms.

Relishing her softness and warmth, David tightened his arms, wanting to kiss her all night through. She trembled, and he didn't think it was from the chilly night. She clung to him, kissing him back wildly, while her hips moved slightly against him, intensifying his desire a thousandfold.

All evening yearning for her had built, growing into a blaze that was all out of proportion to any need he had ever known before. She was beautiful, sexy, alluring, a scalding torment, creating havoc with his thought processes. She was scared of being hurt, but neither one of them was going to fall in love. She talked and kidded him about her schoolgirl crush on him, but he knew she was exaggerating and had gotten over whatever she had felt probably by the time she was thirteen years old.

She shifted slightly and the movement against his body aroused him and sent his temperature soaring. Then she pushed and wriggled away.

"We're in a public place, David. A few more minutes and I'll look too rumpled to go back."

He wanted to ask her again to leave for home, but he knew she was having a good time and he didn't want to spoil her evening in the slightest.

He inhaled deeply, trying to take in cold air to cool his body down and master the urge to reach for her again. She smoothed her dress, which clung to her figure. She looked stunning tonight and he couldn't keep from touching her every minute they had been together.

What would she be like in his arms in his bed? He tried to slam a lid on that thought, knowing he better remember where they were and bank his passion.

"Whatever you want, darlin'."

She smiled at him and reached out to take his hand, and it took a mighty effort on his part to go back inside.

As they returned to the club ballroom, he draped his arm across her shoulders, pulling her close to his side. Moving through the crowd, David faced a tall, platinum blonde who gave him a radiant smile.

"David! How are you?"

"Hi. I'm fine. Cathy, this is Marissa Wilder. Marissa, meet Cathy Grayson."

Cathy smiled broadly at Marissa as the two women spoke, then Cathy turned to chat with David. It took another five minutes before he could politely move on.

"She's beautiful, David," Marissa said. "And you dated her, didn't you?"

"I did, but I don't now," he answered indifferently. He had taken his coat from Marissa's shoulders and slipped into it again. "Jealous?" he teased, and Marissa laughed.

"In your dreams!"

They headed to their table as the band returned to play again. David draped his coat over the back of a chair and held out his hand to lead Marissa to the dance floor. When they moved around the room, he saw Cathy dancing with someone else. Her gaze met David's and she smiled at him and he smiled in return, looking away. A month ago he had thought her appealing and had taken her out. They had had a good time together, but now he felt nothing when he looked at her and he wondered why he had ever been interested. Why did all other women suddenly pale in comparison to Marissa?

He glanced beyond her at the clock. Almost eleven o'clock. At midnight the band would fold and he would get to take her home. How he wished he could take her straight home and make hot, passionate love to her.

He tightened his arms around her, moving slowly, barely dancing, just wanting to hold her close against him. She wrapped her arms around his neck and clung to him and his heart pounded. He wanted her more than he had ever wanted a woman in his life and the realization surprised him.

That sperm bank idea of hers bothered him, needling at him constantly, and he wondered at himself. He shouldn't care what she did. Last month they hadn't known each other. To be correct, he hadn't known her. He had never noticed her before in his life, nor remembered meeting her, although she said he had several times.

This woman had been married. She was earthy, lusty, full of life, enjoying dancing tonight with high enthusiasm. He wanted to take her home, seduce her, make love through the night until dawn. He drew a deep breath as images and fantasies tormented him. Could he seduce her? How strong were those barriers she had around herself—how much did she mean what she said? Her actions told him something entirely different from her words.

He was wound tightly enough to burst with need for her. Images taunted, her touches ignited, her saucy brown eyes challenged.

Until the last slow dance, they danced continually, then he

wung her down in his arms and she had to cling to him as
e leaned over her and kissed her lightly on the mouth. When
e swung her upright again, the band stopped playing and the
ancers headed to their tables.

"You've probably started all sorts of rumors about us. You
now how word flies around town," she said.

"Do you care?" he asked with amusement.

"No, except my sisters are going to start calling and quiz-
ing me tomorrow."

He grinned and put his arm around her waist, pulling her
lose against his side. "Then we might as well give everyone
omething to gossip about," he said, stopping at their table
nd turning her to face him with his arm still around her.

"David!" she exclaimed, pushing out of his embrace. "Not
1 public! Besides, I'm getting looks that could kill from some
f the females in this room."

"That's your overactive imagination. Ready to go?"

"Yes," she said, looking up at him with sparkling brown
yes as they walked out. "This has been an exciting, awesome
ight. It was absolutely enchanting, David."

"That's good, but that isn't what it's been for me."

"You didn't have a good time?" she asked, giving him a
earching look. "You acted like a man having a good time."

"It has been a hot, sexy torment, setting me on fire," he
aid, leaning down to speak softly into her ear.

He watched her inhale deeply and he wanted her so badly
. was an effort to keep from making love to her right there.
nstead, they stepped outside to wait while his car was brought
round to them.

"Well, for me it was a delicious dinner and a grand evening.
love dancing with you, David! Thank you for the night out.
: was just what you said, a great time. And now we'll go back
) real life," she exclaimed, sounding exhilarated.

Her joy was infectious and he was glad she'd had a good
me, but he wanted her to be as hot and bothered as he was.
1ore than anything he wanted her in his arms. He had waited

all evening in anticipation of getting back home and mak
ing love.

As soon as they were in the car, he reached over to tak
her hand in his. "Let's go straight home and pick up Autum
in the morning. Jason and Merry said it would be fine."

"You promised! We're not leaving Autumn all night. Thin
about your first night with her."

"All right. We'll head for the Windovers," David agreec
deciding to pick his battles with her.

"Good." She threw out her arms and sang a line from on
of the songs played earlier and laughed.

She was so bubbly, she couldn't sit still in the car as the
left the club and drove through Royal. "I haven't had an eve
ning like this in I don't know how long!" she exclaimed. "I'ı
sorry I argued about going tonight. It was all you said it woul
be and so much more."

He glanced at her and returned his attention to the road. H
wasn't getting the reaction from her he wanted. He wanted he
hot, wrapped in desire, as ready for passion as he. Suddenl
he had Miss Bubbly Bo-Peep in the car with him, and he ha
to look at her in her slinky black dress to reassure himself sh
wasn't sitting there in that frou-frou ruffled dress.

He reached over to caress her nape, running his fingers bac
and forth lightly.

"I didn't know I could get out and have a good time lik
this ever again, David," she said happily. "For a long tim
there, I never believed I would. But now I know that I can
You know, I guess I can start dating again."

"Damnation," he said fiercely, "you *are* dating, right now
And it's the first time I've taken a woman on a date and she'
talked about how great it would be to date other guys."

"This is different," she said blithely as if they were on tw
different planets. "You said yourself this would just be a care
free evening, pure enjoyment, a one-time deal as I understoo
it. You have proved that I can have a good time getting ou
again, and I'm so thankful, David. Thank you!" she e>

laimed, twisting against her seat belt and throwing her arms round his neck, leaning across the seat to kiss his cheek.

David inhaled, anger, frustration and desire roiling in him while he kept an eye on his driving in spite of her wild hug. He sat in silence when she flounced back into her seat and abbled about dancing and getting out. He wanted all her enthusiasm and passion directed at him, not at the thought of socializing with other guys again.

With each passing mile, his frustration increased. At the next intersection of a county road, he turned, knowing he could get home to the ranch by a half-dozen routes. He pulled off under the shade of a tree, the car bouncing over rough ground and sending a spiral of dust swirling behind them.

"What's wrong? Did you have a flat?" Marissa asked in alarm.

He cut the engine, unbuckled his belt and hers and lifted her across the seat into his arms.

"Dammit, I'm your date, and tonight wasn't that casual!"

"It wasn't?" she asked with wide eyes. "You told me it was. You said—"

"I know what the hell I said, but I didn't mean it as literally as you took it. I wasn't giving first aid to get you in shape to go out with other guys."

"No kidding!"

"Dammit, if you're just trying to yank my chain, you've succeeded."

Her hands were on his forearms, his arms around her as he looked at her in the darkness. Her eyes were huge. She looked truly startled, and he wondered what she really thought. The woman had him tied in knots, something that he couldn't remember ever happening to him before.

"Rissa, come here," he said, and his mouth covered hers, kissing her hard and letting go the need he had bottled up all evening long.

Eight

Marissa's heart thudded as his tongue stroked hers and h held her against him, kissing her as if he were going to devou her.

Her blood heated, all her giddiness and vivacity now chan neled into an impossible craving for the strong man holdin her. The night hadn't been insignificant to her, but she wa trying to keep him from knowing just how deep her longin ran. She thought by sounding as if the evening had been blast and nothing more, she would keep him at a distanc give him the out that he wanted.

She didn't want a broken heart and she didn't want his pit By trying to cling to lightness, she could keep a wall betwee them. Or so she had thought, but his kiss was demolishing th strategy. His kiss was fire and a blatant, unmistakable hung that belied any casual feelings. His kiss was binding, a forev kiss that locked chains around her heart and stormed her wal of resistance. She was disintegrating, coming apart, her desi for him a force she couldn't bank or quell.

She clung to him, kissing him in return, passion bursting into roaring life that broke any idea of a casual relationship into a million pieces.

Dropping her guard, she let all her feelings for him pour into her kisses, trying to burn him to ashes like he was doing to her.

His hands were at the zipper of her dress and he peeled it off and let it fall softly around her waist. Pushing away her bra, his hand cupped her breast while his thumb slowly circled her nipple.

She gasped and moaned, wanting to take off his shirt, but they were crammed into the front seat of his sports car and there wasn't room to move around. She shifted, trying to straddle him, putting a knee on the seat on each side of him.

He slid down her dress and cupped her breasts, taking one into his mouth to kiss her, his tongue circling her nipple. Aching need bombarded her as she tangled her fingers in his hair.

"David, stop," she whispered. "We're out where anyone might drive past." She moved away, pulling up her dress. His uncustomary quietness dawned on her and she glanced at him, surprised to find him watching her solemnly.

"I want you, Rissa, and tonight wasn't casual. It was important."

She inhaled, trying to draw air into her lungs because his words took her breath away.

"Slow down, David. Just go a little slower. I feel like I'm sinking in quicksand here, doing all the things I said I wanted to guard against." She touched his hand, tracing his fingers with her own. "Maybe it's too late for me to hope for caution."

"There's no need for it," David said solemnly.

He reached over to buckle her seat belt, pausing only inches from her to look into her eyes. Her body felt the impact as she gazed back at him. He buckled his own seat belt and started the engine.

She was subdued, curious and far more stirred than she had let him know. They rode in silence and she didn't know whether he was angry or just quiet. She needed to make some decisions—did she want a relationship with David? One that was destined to be temporary?

He reached over to take her hand and place it on his thigh. While she watched him drive, she considered tonight and what she wanted to happen.

They sped through the night, going to the Windovers and picking up a sleeping Autumn and taking her home. David was uncustomarily quiet and Marissa followed his lead, knowing it was just as well.

Tucking Autumn into her crib at home, Marissa was too aware that David stood leaning with his shoulder against the doorjamb while he watched her. As she straightened from bending over Autumn, he motioned with his head.

"Let's go to the kitchen and have a drink."

Did she want to risk her heart again or not? How could she resist him? She crossed the room to go to the kitchen with him.

He built a fire and poured glasses of white wine, carrying them to the sofa.

"Here's to slow dancing and long, hot kisses and to a woman who is changing my life."

"Changing you— I don't think so. And long, hot kisses— you've explored that territory."

"Not like I'm going to," he whispered, taking her glass of wine and setting them both on the coffee table. He turned to take her into his arms, and she closed her eyes as he lowered his head and kissed her.

She wrapped her arms around his neck, telling herself to enjoy the moment. Let go and live. At least tonight. His kiss was fiery, and every touch escalated the need between them. He shifted her to his lap, cradling her against his shoulder, and his hand slid over her, caressing her lightly and then moving to her nape. Deftly, he slipped down the zipper of her dress and peeled it off her shoulders.

Cool air rushed over her heated skin, but she barely noticed anything now except David's kisses. He raised his head, his hands cupping her breasts.

"Rissa, you're beautiful," he whispered before unfastening the simple catch on her black bra and tossing it aside. He leaned forward to take her breast in his mouth, his tongue a delicious torment that heated her. She fumbled at the buttons on his shirt, finally shoving it away to run her hands over his shoulders. She leaned forward to trail kisses along his throat. When her hands played over his chest, he groaned, the sound a faint growl that was lost in their kisses.

She was caught in a whirlpool of emotion, drowning in his kisses, pulled deep into a place she never intended to go, into wanting him desperately. Too swiftly, the great barriers she had around her heart shattered and she was totally vulnerable, unable to resist, wanting him as she had never wanted a man before.

"This isn't fair," she whispered.

"It's fabulous," he replied while he cupped her breasts and kissed first one nipple and then the other. "You're fantastic."

"Words are easy, David," she said, running her hands over him, stroking his warm chest, letting her hands slide down to the bulge in his trousers. He shifted her off his lap and stood, unbuckling his belt while she watched him. As his trousers fell away, he pulled her to her feet.

"David, we—"

Whatever she intended to say was gone, taken by his steamy kiss as he pulled her into his embrace. His hard arousal pressed against her as he held her tightly with one arm banded around her waist. With his other hand, he peeled off her panty hose, then knelt to remove them completely, letting his hands trail over her legs, sliding his fingers up the inside of her thighs while she held his shoulders.

She closed her eyes, her head thrown back, swamped with an aching need when his fingers moved higher.

He stood and his arm banded her waist again. He held her tightly against him while his other hand slipped between her legs, stroking her through the thin fabric of her black lace panties. She gasped and clung to him, lost now, pushed over a brink where all else was forgotten.

His fingers slipped beneath the black lace, stroking her, driving her wild with need for more. He stopped and peeled away the panties as she hooked her fingers in his briefs to free him and then she sat on the sofa, pulling him in front of her to a paradise of discovery, learning the planes and contours of his body. Her tongue slid over him while his fingers tangled in her hair and he groaned again.

Suddenly, he pulled her up, looking at her, and she felt as if she gazed into a bonfire when she looked into his eyes. Longing for him rocked her, and she wrapped her arms around his neck, pressing against him to kiss him hungrily. She was lost, yielding to a longing that had started far back in her past and was stronger than she had ever imagined. Just once with him, ran through her mind. Just this one waltz to paradise with the man that she had always been drawn to.

He picked her up, carrying her to the rug in front of the fire, where he lowered her to the floor and lay beside her. His hands were everywhere, sliding over her, exploring and discovering while she did the same to him.

Relishing every touch, she let her hand slide down his smooth back to his narrow hips, skimming over his tight butt, down over his muscled thighs that were sprinkled with short crisp hair. And then she trailed kisses over him while he kissed her in turn.

He rolled her over on her stomach, straddling her. Firelight highlighted her creamy skin with a pink glow and David's pulse drowned other noises. She was gorgeous, a dream. She said she had waited half a lifetime. It seemed to him that he had waited forever. He was shocked how badly he wanted her but he wanted to seduce her and make her desire him until she felt half the need he did. He leaned down to kiss her nape and then to slowly trace kisses along her back while his hot shaft rubbed over her.

His warm breath was its own caress against her bare skin, his hands sliding across her bottom, followed by his tongue down over the back of her thigh and behind her knee. With a cry she rolled over to pull him down to her and kiss him again.

He lay against her, holding her in his tight embrace, their heated, naked bodies pressed together. His body was bathed in sweat, and he fought to maintain his control. He wanted to love her into oblivion. Her hips moved against him, intensifying his need.

Marissa couldn't get enough of him, she was lost this one night, wondering if she had been in love with him all her life. Enjoy this moment, she told herself. It was once in a lifetime.

The sight of him stole her breath, the feel of him drove her wild. Caressing her, he trailed kisses across her breasts and then down over her belly, down lower. He moved between her legs, pushing her leg up so her knee was bent. When he kissed the inside of her thigh, she opened her eyes to find him watching her, with a hungry, burning gaze.

She shut her eyes again, lights bursting behind her lids as the sweet torment enveloped her. This was David who was kissing her, David who was loving her with a need that demolished her. Her dreams had become reality beyond belief. With every kiss, every caress, each whispered endearment, passion poured from him.

She ran her hands across his shoulders, feeling the smooth, hard muscles in his arms, and then he moved farther between her thighs, trailing kisses where his fingers had been, to her most intimate feminine place. Gasping, she clung to him and thrashed beneath his touch.

"Ah, Rissa, I want you so damned much!" he said in a raspy voice, the words dim with the roaring in her ears as he drove her to a frenzy.

"Are you protected, Rissa?" he whispered, kissing her.

"No, I'm not."

"Then I'll use protection," he said, leaving her and opening a drawer to retrieve a packet. He returned and knelt between her legs.

She drew a deep breath at the sight of him because he was masculine perfection. He was hard, his dark, thick shaft ready for her. His hips were narrow, his shoulders broad, and she drank in the sight of him while his gaze played over her the way his fingers had.

"You're beautiful," he whispered again. He lowered himself, the tip of his shaft touching her, and she raised her hips to meet him, wrapping her long legs around him.

He lowered himself again, his velvety shaft touching her and then moving inside her. Her insides clutched and consuming urgency burst, sending rippling aftershocks through her system. Her thudding heart drowned all sounds as he slowly filled her.

She shifted beneath him, holding him tightly. "David, move, now, love me!" she gasped, knowing she was hopelessly lost.

Sending her into a frenzy, he went slowly, as he withdrew slightly and then pressed into her again. She clung to his broad shoulders, her hips moving constantly while he tried to hold himself in check and make the moment last.

David was enveloped by a need for her softness, her loving, as if he had yearned for that for too many solitary years. Her long legs held him tightly. He looked at her to see that her eyes were closed, and he could dimly hear her whispering his name.

More sweat beaded on his forehead and over his chest and shoulders. It was an effort to hold back, to love her slowly, a hot torment that he wasn't going to be able to curb much longer. She bit her lower lip, catching it with her white teeth.

As he moved with her, passion rocked him, a giddying spiral building that was going to shatter his control.

Marissa clung to David's shoulders, moving her hips against him. "Love me," she whispered, wanting more desperately.

And then his control slipped away and he thrust hard and fast, feeling her match his movements while her arms and legs tightened around him.

Marissa was aware only of his loving, an electrifying need that tore at her. Her body heated, and she wanted him with an unleashed single-mindedness.

Clutching his buttocks as if she could tug him closer, she rocked with him, her body tightening until release burst inside her. She cried out, the release coming, sending her spiraling into a blinding consummation.

"Rissa! Ah, Rissa!"

Dimly, she heard David gasp her name and felt his shuddering release as spasms shook him. Gasping for breath, they both slowed, but then continued moving.

How long was it until she became aware that he was murmuring endearments to her? Time had vanished for her. He trailed kisses along her temple and to her ear.

"My love," he whispered, "Rissa, you're wonderful."

His words thrilled her and she held him tightly, knowing that all too soon reality would return and these past moments would become little more than the fulfillment of an old dream.

Having crashed and burned, they settled back to a calmer world.

"You're a darn, dirty fighter," she whispered, stroking his back.

"And you're a bewitching, sexy darlin', driving me wild and taking me to absolute paradise. Ah, Rissa, what a night! Darlin', it was fabulous."

"I'll have to admit the same," she said, wondering where they would go from here and for a moment not even caring.

He trailed kisses over her face, his arms encircling her. He rolled to his side, keeping her with him, and then his fingers played down her back and stroked her. "You're the most wonderful woman I've ever known."

"You don't really know me at all."

"Yes, I do. I know you have a small mole on your butt."

She ran her fingers over the scar on his shoulder. "What happened here, David?"

"I was shot," he replied tightly, his voice changing. "It was in my line of work."

She raised her head to kiss his shoulder. "What happened to your fingers?" she asked, catching his one hand with hers and tracing his crooked little finger and the finger next to it.

"Broken—in the line of duty."

She shivered and stroked his jaw. "I'm glad I didn't know you then and I'm glad you're not doing that kind of work now."

"Nope, no more military," he said, and she sensed a slight withdrawal in him and wondered what had happened to him that he was keeping to himself. She brushed locks of his black hair back off his damp forehead, finding it fascinating to touch him and equally fascinating just to look at him.

He caught strands of her hair in his hand to let them slide through his fingers. "On your arrival I was shocked when I opened the door and discovered I'd hired a beautiful woman to move into my house."

"I didn't look that different!" she said, smiling at him. "Pigtails and a fluffy dress were about all."

"Hardly," he said. "I couldn't understand why everyone kept telling you that your dress was cute."

"It *was* cute. You just don't know cute when you see it."

"Maybe not, but I know 'sexy' when I see it and feel it," he added, letting his fingers drift down to trail over the curve of her breast.

She caught his hand in hers. "You've already done that."

"If you think that I'm through, you're in for a huge surprise," he drawled. "Let's go get one of those long, warm, leisurely baths together. Lots of bubbles and water and sexy woman."

"I'm surprised. You have a romantic streak in you!"

"I try to keep it hidden," he replied with amusement. He stood and scooped her into his arms to carry her to his large bathroom, where she looked all around. "My goodness, I haven't seen this part of the house before. Don't you get lost in here—it's huge," she observed, looking at the large sunken black-and-gold tub, a shower—a bathroom that would almost hold her bedroom it was so large.

"Not lost, just lonesome."

"I don't believe that one," she said. He stepped down into the tub and sat down with her, then he turned on faucets and opened jars to pour various ingredients into the tub until they were covered in steaming, scented water and suds up to their shoulders. He shifted so she sat between his legs with her back against him. His skin was warm, slippery with water. His legs pressed against hers as he took a sponge to gently soap her.

"Lean forward and I'll rub your back."

She did as he said. "I could purr," she murmured as his hands lightly massaged her back.

He was silent a moment, but she barely noticed, lost in the massage that was relaxing every bone in her body.

"You know, if we dispensed with protection, you wouldn't have to go to the sperm bank."

It took seconds for his words to sink into her lethargic brain. She opened her eyes and turned to slant him a look over her shoulder. His tanned skin was wet and locks of black hair fell across his forehead. His green gaze was inscrutable.

"Is this an offer?" she asked.

"Of sorts," he answered.

"You would be willing to give me a baby and then say goodbye to both me and your child?"

"It's better than you going to a sperm bank."

"Better for whom? How could you do that?" she asked, appalled and becoming annoyed with him.

"You'd at least know the father of your child."

"You'd just bring a baby into the world and abandon it?"

"What do you think you're going to get from a sperm bank?" he asked. "You think a daddy comes with that?" he replied, only half considering what he was saying to her. She was naked, wet, sitting between his legs, her round, enticing bottom pressed against his vital parts, and he couldn't concentrate on their conversation despite it being about the most important subject on earth.

She was breathtakingly beautiful. Her long dark blond hair fell over her shoulders; the ends of wet strands were darker than the rest. She was giving him a look that heated him more than the steaming water. He tossed aside the sponge and slipped his arm around her waist, leaning forward to kiss away her next words.

"Are you listening to me, David Sor—"

His kiss took her words away and then his hands slipped up to cup her breasts as he caressed her nipples. She moaned and twisted around, placing her knees on either side of him. She caressed his hard shaft.

He wrapped his arms around her waist and kissed her, pulling her down on his manhood. She gasped, moving on him as he filled her, slippery, hard and hot, starting another spiral of grinding urgency.

He groaned. "Rissa, love." He ground out the words that she barely heard because of her pounding heart. And then release came, and she felt his frantic thrusts when he climaxed. She clung to him while he turned to kiss her passionately, a long, smoldering kiss that made her wonder about the depth of his feelings.

Remembering, entering reality again, she wondered about him. Would he really care that little about his own baby? Or was that all a cover? Whatever, she wasn't going that route.

She slipped back between his legs and leaned against him while they both gasped for breath. He trailed kisses on her shoulder and her nape, creating more sparks in her in spite of the satisfaction of their lovemaking.

"I'm not sure I would have heard the baby monitor for a few minutes there," she said.

"Oh, yes, you would. Little Autumn has a healthy pair of lungs. You could hear her out in the yard."

After a few minutes she put her head back on his shoulder and he wrapped his arms around her waist to hold her tightly.

"It's a night of paradise," he said in a husky voice.

"That it is," she agreed, twisting her head to look up at him. "Trade places and I'll give you a back rub." They shifted around and she wrapped her legs around him while he sat forward slightly so she could massage his back. She ran her fingers over a scar on his back. "This is the gunshot wound, isn't it?"

"Yes."

She kissed his shoulder and then rubbed his back. "So in a few months you'll move to Houston. Will you come back to Royal?"

"Probably seldom. When I was in the military, I was home very little."

"Home being Royal?"

"Right. I think of this ranch as my home. The house in town is more formal and I never liked staying there as much as living out here."

"Does your father come back to Royal often?"

"I think the last time he was here was about four years ago. He has a home in Houston and one in La Jolla, California."

"When did you last see your dad?" she asked, wondering about the life David led, which seemed in some ways cold and solitary.

"We met in Paris about eight months ago," David answered, his voice deep and his words slow. "Your hands are magic. I think we better get to bed. With your back rub, I feel a sleep attack coming on."

"And Autumn should start crying any moment," Marissa said.

"Can you handle her or shall we draw straws?" he asked, stepping out of the tub and helping her out.

"I'll do it," she replied. "That's what you pay me to do."

He gave her a long look. "I just volunteered to take care of her tonight if you want me to."

"No," Marissa replied, shaking her head. "I'll manage." He handed her an oversize towel and then got one for himself. "Let's dry each other," he said, rubbing her lightly, slowly and sensuously with the soft terry cloth.

"If you keep that up, you won't get any sleep," she said, closing her eyes as he toweled off her breasts with long, light strokes.

"Well, I'm not sleepy now," he answered in his deep voice. She finished drying and dropped the towel in a heap on a marble-topped commode.

In seconds they were in his king-size bed with covers over them and David held her close in his arms, his leg wrapped over hers. "Why don't we turn out the light and get what little sleep we can?"

She agreed, kissing his jaw. He held her close, and in minutes she heard his deep breathing and knew he was asleep. She lay pressed against him, held with his arm tightly around her.

He hadn't been asleep five minutes when Marissa heard Autumn's cry. She slipped out to go to her room and get the baby.

She swiftly yanked on her T-shirt nightgown and then hurried to pick up Autumn. For the next half hour she was busy with the baby, but finally she sat rocking Autumn back to sleep and was left alone with her thoughts.

Memories of the past hours glowed like bright lights in a dark night: dancing in David's arms, his laughter, his kisses, his naked body against hers, their lovemaking. She had to admit to herself that she was in love with him.

But it wouldn't matter. Despite one night in his arms, or even a few nights, she wouldn't get into a long-term relationship with another man like Reed. And tonight David had proved that he was like that with his talk about using him instead of a sperm bank. If he could walk away from getting her pregnant with his baby, he was definitely into casual.

She had seen the women who had come up to him at the country club. Sophisticated beauties. Whatever charm he poured on now, the time would come when he would want a woman like the ones he had always dated. And Marissa was not one of them.

The time would come with David that he would walk out of her life because he was bored with her.

It would hurt to say goodbye to him now, but not like it would if they went into anything long term, not like the pain from the breakup of her marriage. That was true pain that cut deep and was difficult to get over. Even as badly as that hurt, she realized that David's kisses were the best ever. She responded to him more than any other man she had ever known, including her ex. That realization scared her because it made David far too important in her life and she knew he could never be important.

She looked at the precious baby in her arms and cuddled Autumn closer. "Sweet baby. You're a beautiful little baby, a delight. I pray you get to go back to your mommy, but until you do, you have someone who loves you, Autumn. I think you're very special."

The baby slept through Marissa's talking and finally Marissa carried Autumn to her crib and placed her inside. "'Night, little one," she whispered.

"Marissa." The deep voice was behind her.

Startled, she turned to find David watching her from the doorway. He wore his briefs and entered the room, crossing to her. "Will you come back to my bed?"

"I should stay in here, David."

"Then can I stay in here with you?" he asked.

"Yes," she answered, thinking she would enjoy the moment. Soon enough she would see him vanish.

He slipped between the sheets, and as soon as she stretched out, he pulled her into his arms, holding her tightly against his warm, almost totally bare body. She tingled, wanting to turn over and wrap her arms around his neck and kiss him. Instead, she lay quietly, trying to pace her breathing with his, to relax and let sleep come.

"I woke up and you were gone. I don't want you to go," he said, his hand trailing over her, down over her hip. "Will you move into my room?"

His question surprised her only a little. "As always, you're going way too fast. I'm staying in this room for now. We're not rushing into this relationship. It's just temporary, remember?"

"Whatever you want," he whispered, nuzzling her neck. "All I want is to be with you."

His words were temptation and she wanted to yield and take everything he offered, but then she would think of the price that went with it. "No, David. I stay in here, and after tonight, you stay in your room—at least most of the time."

"Whatever you want, Rissa," he said, capitulating too easily, kissing her throat, his hands stroking her.

Before the night was out, he carried her back to his bed and they loved again, but when Autumn woke, Marissa left him to feed and change the baby.

As soon as she had rocked Autumn back to sleep, Marissa climbed into her bed and gazed into the darkness, knowing she was in for a bigger battle than before and knowing she better safeguard her heart as much as was humanly possible. Yet, for a few days, she was going to love David and let him make love to her. It couldn't last, but she was into it now and she wanted this brief interlude to hold in memory. No strings, nothing permanent or lasting—she knew better than to expect that from him. For a time, though, she could relish what they had together.

"Just enjoy the moment," she whispered to herself in the darkness, knowing that was all she could hope for. The sound of David's voice startled her and she frowned and sat up, then slipped out of bed and went to the door of his room.

He thrashed about in bed, speaking nonsensical words, and she realized he was having a nightmare. She didn't know whether to wake him or leave him alone and decided on leaving him alone.

Returning to her bed, she wondered about his past and his injuries that brought that wall up between them whenever she said anything to him about his military life. His shuttered look had made it plain he hadn't wanted to talk about it, yet she wondered what had happened to him and if that caused his nightmare. He grew quiet and she fell asleep.

The next day Marissa realized just how much she had complicated her life the night before.

Nine

Staying on the ranch, Marissa missed church and David worked. Midafternoon, when he returned and charged into the house her heart thumped as if she had just run a mile.

She stood in the kitchen, mixing formula. In his shearling coat, his broad-brimmed black western hat, his long legs in faded jeans, David crossed the room, his boot heels scraping the terra-cotta floor.

"Hi," she said. One look into his scalding gaze and words failed her.

He crossed the room in long strides and swept her up into his arms. "I couldn't wait to see you," he said in a husky voice, lifting her off her feet.

"David," she said, holding out a spoon that dripped with formula. "You'll get formula on you."

"Don't care," he said. He smelled of leather and carried an aura of cold air. "Ah, Rissa, all I've thought about is you," he said, and ducked his head down to kiss her. She felt his hat brim touch her head and then it was gone. Dropping the spoon behind him, she paid no attention when it clattered on the floor. She wrapped her arms around his neck.

His kiss possessed absolutely, making her his woman, binding her to him beyond anything she had ever imagined in her wildest fantasies. She fell apart, boneless, melting, yet giving him back his own.

"Where's Autumn?" he rasped.

"Asleep in her crib." Marissa could barely get out an answer.

While he kissed her again, he set her on her feet and tossed off his coat, letting it fall to the floor. He swept her into his arms, kissing her hungrily as he carried her down the hall to his bedroom. Compelling urgency tore at her as much as his obvious hunger.

Clothes, an obstruction to intimacy, were tossed aside. David caressed her breasts, his hands everywhere, his kisses setting every nerve quivering. She wanted him more than ever, wanted all that he was giving her, his strength, his masculine force, his own special person. Her hands roamed over him, feeling his taut muscles, seeking closeness in a bond that went beyond physical.

He placed her on the bed and moved between her legs, his gaze proclaiming his need as much as his thick shaft. This moment seemed inevitable, as if she had been created to be here at this time, in his arms. And he in hers. It was the pinnacle of dreams, the hard, dangerous drive of reality. This was the man meant for her, a forever love. Whether or not she was the woman for him, she didn't know, but could only hope.

She whispered his name, calling to him, heart to heart. Naked, totally open and giving to the depths of her being because this was where her love was anchored, solid and permanent.

He came down to take her, wrapping his arms around her, and she held him tightly. Broad shoulders, slim waist, hard muscles, a masculine paradigm, yet that wasn't what bound her heart to him now. Her need for him went far deeper, and her bonding with him was for qualities that went beyond the physical.

Entering her, he thrust hard and fast while she raised her hips to meet him, clinging to his strong body as passion carried her aloft.

"David!" she cried out in ecstasy.

"Rissa, love," he whispered.

Rapture burst in her and she knew when he climaxed, knew when he was satiated. In euphoria, she thought that no matter what hurt lay ahead, for this moment in time she was one with the love of her life.

"All I've thought about was you," he whispered, trailing kisses on her throat, her ear, her temple. "I want to devour you. I'd like to spend the next week in this bed with you."

Her heart drummed because she wanted much the same thing, but she wasn't going to admit it to him. "Well, you can't do that. We have to get out of bed to take care of a little baby."

"I know, but that's what I wish. Rissa, you're special," he said, turning on his side and propping his head on his hand to look down at her.

Joy over his words streaked like heat lightning and was gone as swiftly because she knew she shouldn't be taken in by glib words. She raked her fingers through his hair and stroked his jaw, which was covered with dark stubble.

"Next time I'll shave so my beard isn't so rough," he said, running his finger lightly over her lips.

"Next time," she repeated, wondering about him. "David, do you just charge headlong after whatever you want in life?"

"Only when it's really important," he said, giving her a lopsided grin.

She had to smile in return. "Right."

Autumn's cries interrupted them, and Marissa pushed against his chest. "Let me up, and I'll get her."

"I'll take care of her," he said, rolling over and stepping out of bed. "You've been with her all day and I haven't seen her since last night. Unless, of course, you'd take care of her just like you are."

"I'm not running around this house naked!" she snapped, and he grinned.

"Want me to?" he asked.

"No!"

"You don't like my body?" he asked, placing his hands on his hips and standing nude in front of her.

Exasperated with his flirting, she reached out to caress his thigh. "You just want to hear me say it."

His smile vanished, and he inhaled and turned away. "I'll get Autumn," he said, yanking up his jeans.

"Coward," she teased, and he glanced over his shoulder before he left the room, his smoldering gaze holding hers.

"I'll show you how cowardly tonight," he said, and a thrill spiraled down her middle, pooling into heat low in her body. He could excite her with his words, his eyes, his touch.

That night was as magical as the evening before, with David flirting and touching her. Each moment with him was another tie, binding her heart to him, and she knew she was falling deeply in love with the sexy cowboy who had always attracted her.

Late in the afternoon the next day, David drove into town to run errands, stopping briefly by the hospital even though he knew there hadn't been any change.

Ryan was standing guard and David stayed to talk to him a few minutes, but then he left. As he drove through town, he passed a jewelry store. He parked and went inside, self-consciously looking at wedding rings and realizing that the prospect of losing Marissa was something he didn't want to face.

As he drove back to the ranch with a car full of groceries and supplies, he thought about Marissa. She wasn't like any woman he had ever known. Instead of making him satisfied and filling his need for her, their lovemaking had just made him want her more. Was marriage so impossible for him?

He mulled it over because he didn't want her to walk out of his life. She was already too important to him. He couldn't breathe when she entered a room, he was so dazzled by her. He wanted to do anything he could to please her. He had thought he had been in love many times, but he knew now that they were all infatuations. No wonder he had never considered marriage!

The idea of her going to a sperm bank and never marrying, of having someone else's child, or worse, falling in love with another man, tormented him. He didn't want her pursuing any of those options. He didn't know how to have a happy marriage and a big cozy family. She deserved someone who could give her that because that's all she had ever known and that's what she loved.

He clamped his jaw closed tightly as he considered his life. He didn't know anything about regular families—but Marissa did. And he was doing fine with her and Autumn right now. His lifestyle was no longer wild and dangerous.

Would he make a terrible husband or could his love overcome the gaps from his own past? All he knew was that he didn't want to lose Marissa.

The next two days were a blur of passion, heady nights and delightful hours together. Marissa shut her mind to the future, knowing this was a brief idyll, soon to be a memory, yet something she wanted. And instead of his interest slacking, it increased until he grumbled about having to be separated from her at all.

Wednesday night she lay sleeping in David's arms in his big bed when he shoved against her hard enough to wake her. As she rolled over, she heard him talking. He thrashed in the bed, muttering a jumble of words that made no sense to her, and suddenly he sat up gasping, coming totally awake.

As if disoriented, he looked around and then when he saw her, she held out her arms. "Come here, David. Let me hold you," she said.

Wrapping his arms around her, he pulled her close. She slipped her arms around him, feeling his weight on her arm as they lay on their sides. He was drenched in sweat and she wondered what tormented him with occasional nightmares.

"Sorry," he said. "Bad dreams."

She shifted, moving her arm from beneath him and reaching up to stroke locks of his hair off his forehead. "Don't apologize. We all have nightmares sometimes."

He was silent while she kissed his face and ran her fingers through his hair. He took several deep breaths and she knew he was not going right back to sleep. In minutes she felt his arousal as he pulled her closer to hungrily kiss her and nightmares were forgotten while they made love.

More than an hour later they lay locked in each other's arms and she knew in a short time Autumn would wake. Marissa stroked David's back while his fingers played with her hair.

"Rissa, I have this same nightmare occasionally," David said quietly.

"What is it?" she asked, and silence fell again between them while they continued to caress each other.

"It's from the service," he said, beginning to talk so softly, she could barely hear him even though she was close in his embrace.

"When I was growing up, my best friend was Greg Renaldi. The Renaldis lived in Royal and Greg and I were together all through school. We were best buddies, played football. I was quarterback and he was a wide receiver. We went into the service together." David paused, and she waited, letting him tell her what he wanted to in his own time and way.

"A few years ago in one of those little countries in upheaval, I was in a covert operation with Greg when we got caught in a firefight. There were four of us pinned down in a vacant house. Charley Wakeman was killed by a shell that hit the house and set the house on fire. I had been shot."

"That's this shoulder wound, isn't it?" she asked, brushing her fingers lightly over his scar.

"Yes. I was shot and had a broken collarbone and broken fingers," David replied slowly, as if it was an effort to say each word. She waited quietly, letting him tell her how much he wanted to say. "Greg and Cal Hamilton were wounded. Cal Hamilton had been shot in both legs and Greg had a bad wound in his chest and his upper thigh. There were just the three of us, and it was certain death to stay where we were. We were returning fire, but we couldn't hold out much longer.

"Cal and Greg couldn't go on their own, and I wasn't in any shape to get two other men out with me. Time was running out because all of us were injured. Cal and Greg were bleeding badly," David said in a monotone, and she wondered if he had forgotten her presence and was lost in his memories.

"Greg told me to take Cal and go. Cal was drifting in and out of consciousness."

"How could you take anyone with your wound and broken collarbone?"

"You do a lot when you have to. But I couldn't leave my best friend."

"I'm sorry, David," she said, kissing his cheek. He turned to look at her, focusing on her and pulling her close against his chest. She knew he had made it safely home, but she hated to ask him any questions because she knew whatever memories he had, they must be terrible.

"I wouldn't leave Greg," David repeated with anguish in his voice, and then he was silent again for moments before he continued. "Greg pulled out his pistol and put it to his head and told me to take Cal and go or he would pull the trigger."

She tightened her arms around him, hurting for him and realizing what pain he had gone through. "You had to leave your friend behind."

"I left him, but I told him I was coming back to get him. We both knew that was impossible, but I was going to do it."

Marissa held David tightly, wishing she could do something, yet knowing there was no way to ease his hurt.

"I got Cal over my shoulder. As we left the house, I heard a shot."

"Oh, David! It was your friend," she said, aghast at what David had gone through.

"He did it so I wouldn't try to go back to get him," David

said, and his voice broke. She wished more than ever there was some way to stop David's hurting over his loss.

She held him, letting time pass while he got a grip on his emotions, and she realized he probably had never told anyone before what had really happened. "Your friend's family don't know what happened, do they?"

"No. He died fighting for his country. He did it for me, and it wouldn't help to tell them. There was no way to get him to safety. Even if Cal hadn't been there, I don't know that Greg would have survived. He had a terrible wound. Damn, all the common sense in the world tells me that I couldn't have done anything, but I feel I should have saved him." David clenched his fists and she shifted slightly, feeling tears on his cheeks. "I should have saved him or died with him!" he whispered tightly, grinding out the words. "I shouldn't have left him."

"You didn't have a choice when he put a gun to his head. Did Cal live?"

"Yes. He's scarred up, but otherwise fine now," David replied, running his hand across his eyes.

"You can't blame yourself," she said, framing his face with her hands. "You did what you had to and you saved another life. You shouldn't feel guilty for surviving."

"I suppose not," he said, leaning back against the pillows. She leaned over him, running her fingers along his firm jaw, feeling closer to him than she had in their deepest moments of passion.

"That's what your nightmare is about." She kissed his cheek lightly. "Let go of the guilt, David. You did the only thing you could. What would you have accomplished by dying with him? Would he have wanted that?"

"Of course not. I know what's logical, but that doesn't change what I feel in my heart."

"It never does," she replied solemnly, and lay across his chest, holding him tightly, praying that talking about it would be a catharsis for him. "I love you," she whispered, thinking he wouldn't hear her, but his arms tightened around her, and he rolled her over so he was above her.

"Ah, Rissa, I didn't mean to burden you with my woes," he said, his voice lighter.

"I'm glad you told me," she answered, running her finger along his jaw. She wrapped her arms around his neck and pulled him down to kiss him, and in minutes the incident was burned away by passion.

Four days later, David rode with his men, separating cows from calves to take the calves to market. For a while, thoughts of Rissa were driven from his mind as he had to concentrate on what he was doing, but later, when he drove home and saw a section of fence down and stopped to repair it, she filled his mind again.

He worked automatically, thinking about her, fantasizing, hurrying what he was doing so he could get back home to her. They had expected him in Houston at the oil company by mid-November, but without telling her, he had called and postponed his arrival until the first of the year. He had talked to his dad, not even mentioning Autumn or Marissa, figuring he would tell his dad about them when he next saw him.

What a muddle with Autumn and her mother. Poor baby, what could her mother be mixed up in? Possibilities involving so much money and someone after her were chilling.

David twisted wire around a post, but his thoughts went to the nightmare he had had and revealing what had happened to Rissa. It was the first time he had ever told anyone the truth about that operation. There had been no reason to tell anyone and it was too painful to talk about. Nightmares still haunted him and it had been a blessed relief to share the incident with her, but he was surprised that he wanted to. He couldn't ever remember being with a woman he would have told about that time in his life and the pain that it still continued to cause him.

And he faced that fact that Rissa was important to him, different from all the other women he had known. She was special, a fascinating companion and an unbelievable lover. Her responses to him were wild. It hadn't surprised him that she could be totally uninhibited, because she had moments that she told the unvarnished truth regardless of the consequences.

He grinned, thinking about her, but then his grin vanished. Was he in love? He hadn't ever expected to fall deeply in love, not the marry-me-forever kind of love. He didn't know how to have a happy marriage and a big cozy family. She deserved someone who could give her that because that's all she had ever known and that's what she loved.

He couldn't concentrate on work for thinking about her and about what she might do when she left his ranch.

Since when had he been tied in knots if a woman walked out of his life? Since he had known Rissa. He stood up and stared at the fence, seeing only Rissa in his bed.

Was he in love? Marriage. When he thought of it in terms of having Rissa in his life, marriage was beginning to sound fantastic. Silken nights, love and laughter and a best friend forever. But he wasn't what she deserved.

He was going round and round with arguments that got him nowhere. She deserved someone who would be a good father and family man, but David didn't want her marrying that someone. He wanted her to himself.

"Dammit," he said aloud. He turned to his truck. He wanted her and he knew he shouldn't. Sperm bank. "Oh, hell!" he exclaimed, still talking to himself. He wasn't too bad at caring for Autumn. Maybe Rissa could teach him to be a family man. He sat in his pickup and leaned over to stare at himself in the rearview mirror.

"Do I want to get married? Do I want her to go to a sperm bank or marry another guy? Hellfire, no!" he said, sitting straight and forgetting about talking to himself in the mirror. All at once it was imperative to get home to her. He switched on the ignition, slammed the door and headed for the house.

Rissa saw him coming across the yard. Instead of going through the gate, he jumped it easily and she smiled, thinking he radiated vitality and sexiness. Eager to be with him, she rushed to the back door, stepping out on the porch as he took the back steps two at a time and swept her into his arms to kiss her. His kiss set her ablaze and she clung to him, sliding her arms beneath his jacket.

It was cold out, but David was warm, his body hard, and she had waited all day for his return.

While he kissed her, he opened the door and walked them into the house. Still kissing her, he kicked the door shut behind him.

Finally he raised his head. "Marry me, Rissa," he said solemnly. "I love you."

Stunned, she stared at him. "Just like that you want me to marry you? How long have you thought about this? An hour?"

"Long enough to know damned well what I want."

Her heart thudded, and she wanted to fling her arms around his neck and cry yes, but she knew better than to do that. She had been down that road before and knew what lay along it.

"You don't mean it," she said, hurting. She loved him, wanted him, but she had loved and wanted before and got her heart smashed to pieces for it. "And even if you do mean it today, no."

"Why in blue blazes not?" he asked, his hands on his hips, his coat shoved open.

"You don't date women like me."

"What do you mean, women like you?" he asked, his brows arching with curiosity.

"I've seen pictures of the women you date and I know some of them. They're sophisticated. You're like Reed—"

"Stop right there," David interrupted, his eyes narrowing. "I'm not like your ex. Not in any way, shape or form. Forget that foolishness. And as for sophisticated women, I don't know about that. But I do know I don't want to live without you. I don't want you going to a sperm bank and having another man's baby. That ties me in knots. Marry me, Rissa," he said, his voice suddenly dropping and becoming velvety.

She backed away from him. "David Sorrenson, stop! Don't start trying seduction and charm. You're impulsive and headstrong. You just bulldoze your way into getting what you want, like hiring me that morning and seducing me that Saturday night.''

''Seduction was bulldozing?'' he asked, and she thought she saw a twinkle in his eyes.

''David, I'm not marrying you. I mean it. You're not paying any attention to what I'm saying.''

''No, I'm not because I heard you say 'I love you' last night when we were in bed. I know you act like a woman in love.''

''I may be in love with you, but I'm not marrying you!'' she cried.

''Well, if that isn't the most illogical answer I ever got in my life, I don't know what is. If you love me and I love you, why won't you marry me?''

''Listen to me! I know you well enough now to tell that you're hearing only what you want to hear. I will not marry you. This is infatuation. Eventually you won't be happy with me. I'm practical and reliable and can take care of a baby, but sophisticated and worldly and a woman to stir men's passions, I'm not.''

''Like hell. What do you think you've been doing to me every night lately?''

''Will you listen to me! You're exactly like you were that morning. You were determined to hire me whatever you had to do and you did it instantly. Well, this time, get it through your thick, stubborn head, I won't go through a marriage again to a man like you.''

Tears stung her eyes and she whirled away, running for the first time in her life from something that hurt and something she wanted with all her heart.

''Well, I didn't do that right,'' David said to himself, watching her disappear from the kitchen. He hung his hat on a hook and shed his coat to hang it below his hat while his mind churned and he thought about what he could do. He gazed at the empty doorway in speculation.

Marissa stood leaning against her bedroom door, her eyes squeezed tightly shut while she cried. Then Autumn stirred and began to cry. Marissa wiped her eyes, shoving aside her feelings as she picked up the baby to change her. She knew she had to go back to the kitchen to get a bottle for Autumn, but she didn't want to see David yet.

She looked at herself in the mirror. Above her jeans, she wore a red blouse and her eyes now matched it. She wiped at them and shook her hair away from her face, taking a deep breath as she held Autumn close and headed for the kitchen. No matter how much it hurt, she knew she was right. David was like Reed and he would tire of her. Right now, he had to be with her because of Autumn, but the day would come when his interest would wane.

She carried Autumn to the kitchen and was in hopes David was elsewhere, but he was still standing by the sink, gazing out the window. When she entered the room, he turned and crossed to take Autumn from her.

"You've been crying," he said solemnly. Before she could answer, his pager beeped. He handed Autumn back to her and as she got a bottle for Autumn, he picked up his pager.

"I've got to make a call," he said, taking out his cell phone. He punched numbers and in seconds said, "This is David." He was quiet, glancing at her again and inhaling deeply, and she knew there was something important happening.

"I'm at the ranch," he said. "I'll be right there."

He put away his phone and turned to her. "That was Clint Andover from the hospital. Autumn's mother is out of intensive care and in a regular hospital room. She has regained consciousness."

Ten

"**O**h, David!" Marissa exclaimed. "How wonderful!" she said, swamped with relief, yet, at the same time, unable to keep from feeling sad and at a loss. "I'm going to miss Autumn terribly, but that's really good news." She knew she was going to miss David beyond measure also, but she didn't want to tell him.

"We should take Autumn to her. We can get most of Autumn's things to her later," David said.

"You're right. I know she'll want to see her baby as soon as possible. I'll pack a little bag of Autumn's things and you put formula and some bottles in a sack to take."

"I'll feed Autumn while you pack and then you can take her and I'll finish packing another bottle."

Marissa dashed to put tiny baby clothes into a bag, and all the time she packed, she tried to keep from crying. She was losing Autumn and David. She was glad the baby would be reunited with her mother, but it was going to hurt to tell Autumn goodbye. And David was going to break her heart.

In record time they reached the hospital and they rushed to a different room on Jane Doe's new floor.

Clint was standing in the hall with Alex and they turned to meet him. Both were in sweaters and jeans, watching solemnly as David and Marissa approached them.

"We got here as quickly as we could," David said. "This is Marissa Wilder. Marissa, meet Clint Andover and Alex Kent."

As soon as they exchanged hellos, Clint turned to David. "Ryan's on his way," Clint said, and David realized Clint didn't look any happier than he had that first night when Jane Doe had rushed into the diner and collapsed.

"Something's wrong, isn't it? Is she in bad shape?" David asked.

"She's awake," Clint replied, "and they said she's fine physically. She's weak, but okay. The problem is, she has amnesia."

"Oh, hell!" David exclaimed, his hopes shattering that mother and daughter would be reunited and Autumn's mother would be on the mend.

"We're not one step closer to answers now than we were before," Alex remarked. "Here comes Ryan."

They all turned as Ryan strode down the hall, his jacket swinging open. He wore jeans and a navy shirt beneath his jacket. "What's the news?" he asked as soon as David had introduced Marissa. "I thought you'd all be in there with her."

"The doctor is in there right now," Clint said. "Ryan, they say she's conscious, but she has amnesia."

"No!" He looked at the other men. "That leaves us nowhere. She can't take her baby yet, can she?"

"Nope. She's staying longer in the hospital. She doesn't remember anything, so she won't know friend or foe. She's as vulnerable as ever," Clint said. "Keep taking care of little Autumn, David."

"Sure. We'll be happy to," he said, looking at Marissa, who nodded. "Does the doctor have any idea about the amnesia and how long it might last?" he asked.

"No. The doctors who've seen her are at a loss. They hope it's temporary, but they can't give me a definite prognosis. So we're still at square one."

"I don't have any news," Alex added, frowning. "I can't trace the names on that list she had. I don't know whether they're fake names or what, but I'm not coming up with anything."

"So the mystery woman remains a mystery," Ryan said.

"Sorry I got you all up here," Clint said. "When I found out she was regaining consciousness, I made my calls. The doctors and nurses were in a flurry and none of us knew anything certain. If I'd known, I wouldn't have brought everyone here on the run."

"That's okay," Alex said. "You didn't know, and if she'd been all right, all of us would have wanted to be here."

"Have you talked to her doctor about letting her see her baby?"

"No. When Tara gets here, I'll ask her, and she can find out for me. I'm sure they'll want her to know about her baby. That might trigger something. Probably tomorrow, David. How will that be?"

"Fine. There's no need in us waiting around here. We'll leave and as soon as you talk to Tara and know when you want us back, just give me a call."

They left and went to eat while they were in town and went by Marissa's house for a couple of hours while all the Wilder females hovered over Autumn. David got a call from Clint, asking him to return the next morning with Autumn.

After leaving the Wilders' house, as soon as they reached the ranch, Autumn stirred and needed a bottle. Marissa got one and disappeared into her room with the baby, closing the door and shutting David out for the night.

Less than twenty-four hours later, David and Marissa entered Royal Memorial again, this time with Autumn in her carrier. The baby was awake, looking wide-eyed at her surroundings.

Clint Andover and Tara Roberts were waiting to meet them. "Good morning," Tara said, stepping forward to look at Autumn. "Let me see her baby," Tara said, her voice softening. "How's little Autumn today?"

Brushing away curly tendrils of her own blond hair, Tara leaned down to look at Autumn who was in a pink sweater. Beneath it she wore a pink dress and booties. "She's a beautiful baby," Tara said, straightening up and looking at David with worry clouding her green eyes. "Jane Doe doesn't remember her baby or anything else, but we've told her that she has a baby girl and that friends of Clint are caring for her." Tara glanced at the room and then back at them. "If you'll please wait a minute, I'll tell her you're here."

"Would it be better if you take Autumn in?"

"I think you and I both can, Marissa," Tara replied. "I'll tell her." In seconds Tara stood in her patient's doorway and motioned for Marissa to join her. David handed Autumn to Marissa.

Marissa entered the sunny hospital room. Jane Doe was propped up in bed, looking stronger and healthier than when Marissa last saw her in ICU. Her violet eyes were large, glancing at Marissa and then going to the bundle in her arms.

"This is Marissa Wilder," Tara said cheerfully. "Marissa, meet our Jane. And this is your baby, Jane."

"This is Autumn," Marissa said, moving close to the bed. "That's the name you called her the night you came to Royal." Marissa held out Autumn.

"Autumn," Jane said softly. Tears came to her eyes, spilling over, and she held out her arms to take the baby. Marissa felt a tight knot in her throat, hurting for the mother who didn't know her own baby, yet who so obviously wanted to know her.

Jane Doe took Autumn, holding her close in her arms. "Autumn. My Autumn," she repeated with awe. "She's beautiful."

"She's a good baby," Marissa said. "So easy to take care of. She's precious. I brought her bottle because it's almost time to feed her and I thought you might want to." She handed a bottle to Autumn's mother.

"Oh, yes! Thank you," Jane said, looking up at Marissa, and Marissa felt a bond, knowing that Autumn bound them together in a friendship that needed no other reason to exist.

"I'll leave you alone with her for a while," Marissa said. "Tara can bring her out to us." Impulsively, Marissa squeezed the mother's thin hand. "Maybe it won't be long now until you remember. You've come a long way already."

Jane wiped her eyes and smiled at Marissa. "I can never thank you enough for taking good care of her for me."

Marissa nodded, not trusting herself to speak while tears still spilled out of Jane's luminous violet eyes and she held Autumn close in her arms.

Marissa quietly left the room, wiping her eyes and crossing to David. One look into his eyes and he reached out, pulling her into his embrace and just holding her while she gathered her emotions together.

In minutes he released her, and she took a deep breath. "They may be a while."

David nodded and Clint motioned to benches where they could sit and he could still watch Jane Doe's room. For an hour they sat and talked until Tara appeared with Autumn in her arms.

"Autumn's asleep now, and Jane said to bring her back to you," Tara said, giving Autumn to Marissa. "Thanks for bringing the baby. That may have helped even though there's no change right now. It made her a lot happier, I know that."

David buckled Autumn into her carrier, and they told Clint and Tara goodbye, taking the stairs and walking down a wide, empty hallway toward the lobby.

"How terrible it must be for her to know this is her baby and yet not remember anything and to see her child leave with a stranger."

"Mr. Sorrenson!" a woman called, and David turned to see a nurse hurrying toward him. "Mr. Sorrenson, Mr. Andover asked me to catch you. He wants to see you again before you leave.''

"Sure."

"I'll just wait here with Autumn, David," Marissa said, motioning toward an upholstered bench along the wall.

He nodded and was gone, his long legs covering the distance swiftly as he went back to take the stairs. While the nurse left and a woman passed with a clipboard, hurrying out of sight, Marissa put the carrier beside her. Down the hall a door opened and an orderly came toward her.

"Miss Wilder?" he asked.

She stood, looking into cold blue eyes as he extended his hand. "We'd like Jane to see her baby one more time."

"Of course," Marissa said, picking up the carrier.

He reached for the carrier. "I can take her, and you can just wait."

"I'll carry her," she replied. The man smiled, nodded and dropped his hand to his side as they headed toward the elevator. Marissa's skin prickled, and without any justification except the fact that he had tried to take Autumn away from her, she didn't want to get into the elevator with him.

"Let me call my friend and tell him we're going to Jane's room because he expects to find us right here," she said. She glanced down the hall and realized the area she was in was deserted at the moment.

She placed the carrier on her arm so she could get her phone from her purse, but the man suddenly pushed her, reaching for the carrier and trying to yank it from her grasp.

Doubling her arm up, Marissa held the carrier close while she swung the diaper bag with all her strength and screamed as loudly as possible.

She saw his fist coming and tried to duck, but failed, taking a blow that made stars dance before her eyes.

When he grabbed the carrier, Marissa still held it tightly in the crook of her arm, close against her body. Screaming, she kicked him.

Eleven

David strode up to Clint, who was talking to Tara. "You wanted to see me?"

Clint's brows arched. "No."

"You didn't send someone—" David's words broke off and he whirled around to run. "Guard that door, Clint, and call security!" he yelled as he raced back toward the stairs.

He skipped stairs, barreling down two flights. At a landing, he heard screams. He jumped the last of the stairs, landing on his feet and yanking open the door. Marissa wasn't where he left her, but then she screamed again and as he spun around, a man ran down the hall.

Marissa waved her hand. "We're all right. Get him!"

David raced after the man streaking away. He disappeared through a door and was lost to sight.

Hospital personnel were appearing, popping out of doors while a security guard ran toward David. David ignored all of them, running as fast as he could and slamming through a door to run down a hallway. Doors were everywhere, one leading to stairs, another outside.

Desperately, David opened and closed doors and finally gave up in disgust, turning around to go back to Marissa, who was surrounded with people, Tara and a security guard at her side. Nearby stood the nurse who had told David that Clint wanted to see him.

"I lost him," David said as he moved close and swore under his breath. Marissa was holding a cold compress against her cheek. "That bastard hit you."

"I'll recover," she said, looking at David and amazed by the change in him. He looked angry and dangerous, with a glint in his eyes she had never seen before, and she realized there was a dark, tough side to him. "The main thing is that Autumn is safe."

"Yes, that's important," David said. He saw Autumn was fine, gazing around in contentment. "But, dammit, I hate it that he struck you."

They talked to the security guard, met Carrie Dunn, the nurse who had told David that Clint wanted to see him. She was baffled, saying a man told her he was Clint Andover and would she go get David Sorrenson before he left the hospital. She knew Clint was the main guard for Jane Doe so she did as the man asked.

She gave them a vague description, saying she paid little attention to him at the time.

Taking Autumn, and joined by Tara, David and Marissa went back upstairs to talk to Clint, and in minutes, Wayne Vicente showed up to ask them about the man.

"Marissa has the best description," David said, and the chief listened as she described the stranger.

"He had blue eyes," she said, glancing at Autumn to reassure herself that the baby was safe. "He's blond and about as tall as David. He was strong."

"The guy Clint tangled with was strong, tall, lean," David added.

"Thanks," the chief said. "I have men combing the

grounds, but this is a big place on a main thoroughfare. He could be hiding in the hospital or long gone.''

They spoke for a few more minutes and finally David and Marissa were alone with Clint.

''Well, now we know that he's out there,'' Clint said. ''He knows our names and he seems to be after both the baby and the mother.''

''He probably wants that money that Alex put in safekeeping,'' David said. ''Clint, we need to have a meeting tomorrow. I'll call the others and we'll put Autumn on a twenty-four-hour watch. She'll be safe, I promise you.''

''Good. I better get back upstairs. One of the cops is up there now guarding Jane Doe's room. How'd you keep the guy from getting Autumn?'' he asked Marissa.

''I just wouldn't let go,'' Marissa said. ''Besides, I hit him with the diaper bag and it has a can of formula and another bottle of milk in it, and I kicked him, too. But I think my screams were what sent him running.''

''Well, I'm glad you were here, though I'm sorry you got punched. Take care, and I'll keep up my guard,'' Clint said.

''I'll look great for Thanksgiving dinner,'' Marissa told David, touching her face gingerly.

''You'll heal or cover it with makeup,'' David said, putting his arm across her shoulders protectively. ''Good job, darlin'. You handled that like a pro. But then I'm not surprised,'' he said, looking at her with obvious admiration.

''I wasn't giving up Autumn.''

''Well, you did a damn fine job of protecting her. I'm impressed.''

''It was desperation or determination. I don't know which. David, can your friends keep the mother safe?''

''Yep. They'll be very careful and they definitely are not afraid of this guy. We all want to catch him.''

As they rode back to the ranch, Marissa studied David, knowing there was another tough side to him. And knowing that every day now they would draw closer to parting and she was going to miss him beyond measure. Being with him was exciting and, at the same time, the most natural thing on earth. She didn't want to tell him goodbye, yet she couldn't consider the alternative. Or could she?

When they reached the ranch, Marissa carried Autumn to her room to change her and then held her close while she went to get a bottle. Still in jeans and a blue, short-sleeved sport shirt, David stood at the kitchen window, drinking a glass of milk when she entered. He held out a bottle he had readied for Autumn and followed Marissa as she carried the baby to the rocker.

"Will you go to dinner with me tonight?" he asked.

"I don't think so, I'd rather stay right here," she replied, looking out the window and trying to avoid his eyes.

He crossed the room, placed his hands on the arms of the rocker and knelt down in front of her, pressing against her knees. She had to look around at him. "Please, Rissa, go to dinner with me."

"If we go out, won't we just argue?"

"No, we're going to eat and have a good time." He gazed up solemnly, but why did she have the feeling he was holding back laughter?

"This is one time you're not getting your way," she said.

"About going to dinner or about getting married?" he asked.

"About getting married," she replied.

"Great! You'll go to dinner with me," he said, standing up. "Seven. I have to run an errand. I'll get one of the guys to come up to the house since you're here alone with Autumn."

"David, don't get a baby-sitter to take care of me! And I didn't say I would—"

"All right," he interrupted. "No sitter, but I'll get him to hang around outside. Darlin', I'll see you at seven and I'll get the Windovers to keep Autumn."

He was gone, striding across the room, grabbing his hat and coat and heading toward the door.

"David, I didn't say I would go to dinner—"

"You'll have a good time. I promise. I'll be back in plenty of time." He rushed out of the kitchen and she heard the back door close and the lock click.

"David Sorrenson, you're bullheaded, arrogant and pushy!" she shouted. "And wonderful," she added in a soft voice. She realized she was rocking furiously and slowed, holding Autumn while her emotions churned.

He had shared himself in every private, intimate way possible with her and her alone and maybe she was wrong about the kind of woman he wanted or needed. And maybe she was being blinded by the past.

Marry him! Her heart cried out what she wanted with all her being.

She spent the afternoon in a storm of mixed emotions, finally bathing for their date, laying out the black dress again, wondering if they would go to the Texas Cattleman's Club for another evening of dining and dancing.

She bathed and dressed Autumn in soft pink frilly pajamas and wondered where David was. While she was getting dressed, she heard him come into the house.

"Hi, darlin', I'm home," he called. He passed her room and knocked.

"Just a minute. I'm dressing," she called, pausing with panty hose in her hands. She wore black lace panties and a black bra.

The door swung open and he thrust his head inside. He whistled as he looked at her. "I promised dinner or we could just stay right here. You look luscious."

"When I said I was dressing, that was not the same as saying 'Come in,'" she snapped, yanking up the dress to hold it in front of her. He grinned.

"I'll be ready in ten minutes," he said, and closed the door.

She picked up a pillow and threw it at the door, feeling excitement and an inner turmoil because, for the first time, she was facing what life would be like without him. And thinking about his proposal all over again.

Ten minutes later when she left her room, she found David

waiting in the kitchen. With his black hair neatly combed and his jaw clean-shaven, he was incredibly handsome in a charcoal suit with a red tie. He smiled at her and took Autumn from her to get the baby into her carrier.

On the way to the Windovers and later, through the drive to Royal, David was charming, never broaching the subject of marriage, yet it was foremost in her thoughts. Was she making a mistake by lumping David with Reed, attributing the same playboy attitudes to both?

They ate in a quiet secluded corner of Claire's, Royal's elegant French restaurant. A pianist played across the room, soft music wafting on the air. Over flickering candlelight they ate steak dinners while David poured out the charm until she was tingling, aching with desire for him, wanting to return to the ranch and to his arms.

"We can go dancing or go home," he said finally. They had long ago finished dinner and had been sitting talking for the past hour.

"I'd rather go home," she said, seeing her desire mirrored in his green eyes.

He inhaled and stood, coming around to hold her chair and help her into her black coat.

He drove swiftly through the cold, dark night. A wind had sprung up and whipped leaves into the air, blowing weeds along the road, but it was cozy and warm in the car. He talked about the ranch and Autumn and related funny anecdotes about his life, asking her about her family while the miles sped by. All the time she talked and then in moments of silence, she kept wondering if she was seeing David in his true light. Was she letting her past heartaches and fears blind her to something wonderful in her life right now?

The question was a torment because Jane Doe should soon recover fully and then Marissa knew she would no longer be needed.

Then she realized they were turning into David's ranch.

"David, we have to get Autumn."

"We will," he replied. "I just wanted to stop and show

you something." He drove halfway to the house and then turned on a path across an open field. The path was barely two faded ruts across rough ground and the car bounced continually, jarring her teeth and her spine.

"Where on earth are we going? You're going to tear up this sports car. I don't think it was meant for this kind of terrain."

"It sure as hell wasn't, but it's the only way to get us where I want to go tonight," he said, and she wondered what he intended to do.

He finally drove up a sloping hill, the car spitting dirt and weeds out behind them as it bounced and lurched over uneven ground. "David! Shouldn't we get out and walk?"

"We're almost there." He reached the top of the hill and stopped beneath a tall oak. Cutting the engine, he climbed out and came around the car to open her door. "Come here, Rissa."

He took her hand and slammed the door behind her. Pulling her coat close around her while wind whistled through the treetops and whipped against them, she looked around. There were thick bushes to one side, a stack of boulders to another, and she couldn't imagine where he was going. Taking her with him, he walked to the far side of the oak where the land dropped away and she could see a huge expanse of the ranch.

"This is a high spot on the ranch and it's kind of secluded because of the trees and bushes and rocks."

"So it is," she said, holding her coat close under her chin as cold wind buffeted her.

"I wanted you to see it because when I was a kid, like nine or ten—I don't even remember—I used to come up here and look at this ranch and think that when I grew up I'd marry and have a real family and live here on the ranch. I didn't have a real family, Rissa, and I wanted one," he said, turning to her. "This was my special place to dream about the family that I might someday have."

"Oh, David," she said, imagining him as an only child,

lonesome, missing a mother and coming here alone, yet aware he was blatantly playing on her sympathy to get his way.

"I've never brought anyone here before, never told anyone about this place. Rissa," he said, brushing a kiss on her temple, "I can tell you anything. I've told you my deepest secret. I didn't think I could ever marry because I didn't know how to be a family man, but with you, I think I can. I just don't want to let you go."

"David!" she gasped, torn between old fears and her new love. His words thrilled her and she wanted to believe him. Could she bury the past and its heartaches, and trust David now?

"I've led a dangerous life, one that wasn't meant for a family man. But I'm out of that now. Rissa, you're important to me."

"David—"

"Don't tell me that I'm just saying that. I mean it. You're more important than anything on earth." He reached into his pocket and fished around, withdrawing his hand. He took her hand and slipped a ring on her finger.

"Marry me, Rissa. I love you and I need you. I don't want to let you go."

Wind buffeted her and leaves blew past them. "Oh, David!" she exclaimed, her heart pounding. She loved him and maybe had loved him all her life.

"I'm proposing. Will you marry me, Marissa?"

Wrapping her in his arms, he said, "I need you. I love you. I want you, only you, and I'll do everything I can to be the right kind of husband and father and family man. When I don't know what to do, you can teach me. You're the perfect woman for me—nurturing, passionate and trustworthy. Marry me, Rissa."

His words were golden promises. She loved him and didn't want to think about a future without him.

"Yes," she said, feeling like this was right and true and she wasn't making a mistake. She had dreamed of this moment while never expecting it to really happen. And she would let go of memories of her first marriage and cling to the present.

"Rissa!" he exclaimed with so much love in his voice that it was plain to hear.

Her heart thudded as he leaned over her and held her so tightly she could barely breathe. Her senses swam and her heart pounded and she wanted him with all her heart.

His head dipped down and he kissed her, pouring his feelings into his kiss, making her tremble with need as his kiss gave credence to his promises, shattered all her qualms and set her pulse racing, a hungry, joyous kiss that built a bonfire of longing.

Suddenly he released her and let out a whoop. "Ye-haw!" he shouted, and swung her up in the air. "Mrs. David Sorrenson. Darlin', how I love you! Let's go tell your family and we'll call my dad!"

She laughed, clinging to his strong arms. "David, put me down."

"I'll put you down, but I promise I'll do my damnedest to never let you down," he said, setting her on the ground again and looking at her solemnly. "I don't want to go through life without you. I need you badly."

"I love you, David," she said, her heart brimming with joy.

He kissed her again, a long, slow kiss that was another deep promise of love. And she held him tightly, feeling sure and right about her decision.

"Let's get in the car so I can look at my ring," she said, caught up in the excitement. "I want to enjoy the moment to the hilt now."

He laughed and took her hand and rushed to the car, holding open the door. She held out her hand in the light of the car and looked at the enormous diamond on her finger as it sparkled.

"Oh, David, it's beautiful! When in heaven's name did you get it?"

"That's what I had to run out of the house for this afternoon."

"Oh, my word! I'll bet you browbeat and bribed some jeweler to get this in a rush," she said, knowing from his wide grin that she spoke the truth. Her smile vanished. "This means I have to move away from Royal and go live in Houston."

"No, it doesn't, darlin'. I've been thinking about what you said about staying on the ranch. That's what I'm going to do. I'll break the news to my dad."

"That's wonderful!" she cried, flinging her arms around him and kissing him, a kiss that she had meant to be brief, but turned into a long, scalding embrace that had them both shaking. When he opened her coat and pushed her down on the car seat, she shoved against his chest.

"No, you don't! We're not making love up here in the car in the freezing cold. You take me home and we'll come back in the summertime."

"Is that a promise?"

"Yes!" she cried, laughing with him as he helped her up and she went around to get into the passenger side of the car.

"Let's go, Mrs. Sorrenson-to-be."

She slid into the car and watched him get behind the wheel.

Thanksgiving Day they sat around the Wilder table at Marissa's parents' home in Royal. As her father carved the turkey, David reached beneath the table to take her hand and give it a squeeze.

She felt too bubbly and excited to eat. Tomorrow was their wedding, tonight the rehearsal. She looked around the table at her sisters, all of Karen's family, their grandmother and her parents, who had flown home for Thanksgiving and her wedding. She glanced at her handsome fiancé who sat beside her. Next to him, was his father, Jerome Sorrenson, a distinguished man with touches of gray in his black hair at his temples. Beyond him at the end of this side of the table Autumn was sleeping in a baby swing.

Joy filled Marissa, and she prayed that she and David would have the same happiness her parents had found in each other.

She squeezed David's hand in return and then had to release him as a plate was passed to her.

Over a bountiful turkey dinner with all the trimmings, conversation filled the room.

"Well, I can see now why I'm losing you in Houston," Jerome Sorrenson said, smiling at David.

"We'll visit, Dad," David replied.

"And you visit us," Marissa urged.

"That I'll do. At least I'll know the ranch is in good hands." He looked around the table at the Wilders. "You're getting quite a family, David. It's wonderful."

"And Louise Wilder can match you in chess," David said, stirring up a flurry of conversation about a future chess match between his dad and Grandma Wilder.

That night after the wedding rehearsal and a party at a friend's of the Wilders, David's father left for his house while the rest of them returned to Marissa's parents' house, where David stayed for about an hour and finally told them goodnight.

Marissa followed David to the door. As soon as she stepped outside with him, he pulled her into his arms to kiss her.

"Tomorrow afternoon," he said finally, raising his head, "you'll be my wife, Rissa. I promise you that when Autumn is reunited with her mommy, we'll take a month-long honeymoon to make up for not having one now."

"As long as I'm with you, I'm happy. I could have told you that in the store that first morning."

He smiled and stroked her cheek lightly. "I love you, darlin'. And I love your family. They're great."

"They love you, too."

"They barely know me."

"They love you because I love you and Grandma and my sisters know you and like you."

He laughed. "Just as long as you love me. It'll be good, Rissa."

"You'd better go. I'll see you in church tomorrow." She

watched him stride away and still was dazed with the idea that she would be his wife. Tomorrow at noon she would become Mrs. David Sorrenson.

The next day, an hour before noon, Rissa stood in the church dressing room while her bridesmaids bustled around her and her mother held Autumn. In a knee-length white silk dress and her hair piled high on her head, Marissa was joyous and eager. She touched the diamond pendant that had been a wedding gift from David, a token of the promises he had made to her.

They had tried to keep the wedding simple with only closest friends and family, but still, they had filled the chapel with guests. In a dreamlike state Marissa watched while each of her sisters, carrying a single rose, walked down the aisle to stand with her.

And then Marissa stepped to the door to take her father's arm. In his navy suit David stood at the front of the church with his friends beside him. She knew the groomsmen now, Jason Windover, Alexander Kent and Chet Renaldi who was Greg's younger brother. Her gaze flew back to David as the small collection of close friends and relatives stood and a friend played a violin. When she walked down the aisle, Marissa's attention totally focused on the man who had captured her heart so long ago.

Taking and holding David's hand and looking into his green eyes, she repeated her vows and finally David kissed her lightly. The minister pronounced them man and wife, magical words, binding them forever.

Many more friends were invited to the reception party at the Texas Cattleman's Club where Marissa danced the first dance with her new husband. "I love you," she said, looking up at him. "I can't believe this isn't a dream."

"I'll convince you it isn't, Mrs. Sorrenson," he said. "That sounds good to me—Mrs. Sorrenson. How long before we can cut that cake and get out of here? I want you all to myself."

She laughed. "Patience! Something you don't know much about."

"*Au contraire, chérie.* I can be as patient as Job."

"Give me one example."

"Waiting to get you naked in my arms today. I'm showing extreme patience with all this."

She laughed. "But fussing every second about it."

He grinned and tightened his arm around her, feeling like the luckiest man on earth. He liked her family and was relieved that they seemed to like him and his father. He looked across the room at his father talking to Aaron Black.

"Your family is willing to take Autumn tonight even though they know it may put them at risk?" David asked again.

"Can you imagine anyone trying to tangle with all my family at once?" she said. "Grandma is staying at my folks' tonight, so they'll all be under one roof. And Mom and Dad are keeping Autumn in their room. My dad is used to dealing with mean animals. He can deal with a mean human if he has to."

"I'm not worried. I agree with you. I'm just trying to plot our escape from this shindig."

It was two hours before David could get Marissa away. He drove swiftly to the airport, where they took a private jet to New Orleans. In a hotel in the French Quarter, they had the bridal suite.

The night air was warm. Street musicians sent music spinning into the darkness. When David tipped the bellman and closed the door behind him, turning to her, Marissa's heart pounded with excitement. David caught her hand and pulled her to him.

"Come here, darlin'. Mrs. Sorrenson. I feel like I've been waiting forever for this moment."

"You think you've waited long! David Sorrenson, I've been waiting since I was eleven years old. And now all those dreams have finally come true. Kiss me and let me make sure it isn't a dream."

"Anything to keep my wife happy," he said, dropping his coat on a chair and pulling her into his arms. Marissa wrapped her arms around his neck, holding him tightly, her heart filled with wonder and joy as she turned her face up for a kiss from her husband, the man she had always loved and would always love in the future.

"Give us a baby, David," she whispered.

"Anything to make you happy, Rissa," he said, tightening his arms around her to kiss her thoroughly.

Happiness warmed Marissa as she held her husband tightly against her heart and prayed that their life ahead would be filled with love and laughter and babies.

Leaning back, she looked up at him. "Enjoy the moment, David," she said, laughing, and he smiled in return.

*　*　*　*　*

Watch for the next installment of the
TEXAS CATTLEMAN'S CLUB:
THE STOLEN BABY
*Texas bachelor Clint Andover is a security
expert who's sworn off love. When nurse
Tara Roberts began receiving threats, he was
determined to watch over her. But in keeping
Tara out of harm's way, would he risk losing
his heart?*
LOCKED UP WITH A LAWMAN
by Laura Wright
*Coming to you from Silhouette Desire
in December 2003.*
*And now, for a sneak preview of
LOCKED UP WITH A LAWMAN,
please turn the page.*

One

"**N**urse Roberts actually took our Jane Doe home!" Clint shot his TCC buddies a stormy glance before dropping into one of the leather armchairs in the meeting room at the clubhouse. "And after I gave her express instructions——"

Ryan Evans glanced up from his game of pool with David Sorrenson, and snorted. "You gave a woman instructions?"

"Yes."

"And you actually thought she'd comply?" Alex Kent asked with a grin, pouring himself a brandy.

Clint frowned, growling back, "I don't see the problem."

"Take it from a happily married man who wants to stay happy." David turned around, the late-afternoon sun blazing in behind him from the windows. "*Never* give a woman instructions."

Shaking his head, Ryan muttered, "Happily and married in the same sentence. What happened to you, man?"

"Just wait, Evans," David shot back as he turned back to

the table and quickly sent one of his solids into the right corner pocket. "Your time's coming."

"Not possible." And with that, Ryan missed his next shot.

David chuckled. "Looks like your confidence is waning there, buddy."

"You're such an ass," Ryan muttered, his dark eyes glinting with irritation.

"Can we get serious, gentlemen?" Clint looked from one man to the other. "I have a problem here."

Alex dropped into the chair beside him. "Does this nurse know about our attempted break-in?"

"To Jane's hospital room?"

Alex nodded.

"No."

"What about the grab on Autumn?" David asked.

Clint shook his head. "She only knows what everyone else knows. The news reports of Jane collapsing at the diner and that Autumn is her child."

David shrugged. "Maybe you should tell her the rest."

"I don't think that's a good idea."

Alex nodded. "The less the people of Royal know about the dangers of this situation the better."

"I agree," Clint replied. "But without revealing that bit of information, I have little chance of getting Tara to bring Jane back to the hospital."

"Well," Alex began, fiddling with his glass, "looks like you might have to guard our Jane Doe from the nurse's house then."

A ripple of heat gripped Clint's chest at the thought of sharing space with Tara Roberts, but he brushed it off. Sure, he was attracted to the pretty blond nurse—had been since school—but this was business. And he never mixed business with pleasure. "Protecting Jane from Nurse Roberts's house?" Clint shook his head. "Easier said than done."

"Why's that?" Alex asked.

"Tara's a pretty stubborn—"

"Pretty and stubborn, huh?" David interrupted, his grin crooked. "Sounds interesting."

Clint shot his friend a dry glare. "It's nothing like that, Sorrenson. Tara and I are...well, we're just old friends."

Ryan lifted a brow. "No kidding."

"We've known each other since junior high."

"First brush with lust?"

When Clint didn't answer, just sneered, Ryan chuckled. "Sounds serious."

"How can it sound like anything?" Clint countered icily. "I didn't say a word."

Pool cue in his right hand, Ryan pointed the cube of blue chalk in his left at his friend. "That's why it sounds serious."

"We talking about puppy love here, Andover?" David asked, grinning broadly.

Clint's chest tightened, and for a moment his mind blurred as the images of that night, of Emily, of fire and death, of all of it, threatened to choke him. He didn't want to hear words like *love* tossed in his direction ever again, and he made his position crystal clear as his voice went low and menacing. "I've loved just one woman in my life."

The men sobered instantly. David and Ryan returned to their game, while Alex drained his brandy.

Coming to his feet, Clint paced the length of the Oriental rug. "There is nothing here and never will be. Tara and I are locked in a battle of wills, that's all. And it's about time I took control of the situation."

Alex nodded solemnly. "What do you plan to do?"

"Jane Doe can just as easily stay at my place as Tara's. Hell, they can both stay there if that's what they want. But our mystery woman will have my round-the-clock supervision regardless."

"Just as long as you realize that you might have a fight on your hands," Ryan offered.

"Maybe so," Clint said, rising to his feet at the challenge. "But it's a fight I fully intend to win."

*　*　*　*　*

✂ **Your opinion is important to us!** Please take a few moments to share your thoughts with us about your experiences with Harlequin and Silhouette books. Your comments will be very useful in ensuring that we deliver books you love to read. *Please take a few minutes to complete the questionnaire, then send it to us at the address below.*

Send your completed questionnaires to:
Harlequin/Silhouette Reader Survey, P.O. Box 9046, Buffalo, NY 14269-9046

---

1. As you may know, there are many different lines under the Harlequin and Silhouette brands. Each of the lines is listed below. Please check the box that most represents your reading habit for each line.

Line	Currently read this line	Do not read this line	Not sure if I read this line
Harlequin American Romance	❑	❑	❑
Harlequin Duets	❑	❑	❑
Harlequin Romance	❑	❑	❑
Harlequin Historicals	❑	❑	❑
Harlequin Superromance	❑	❑	❑
Harlequin Intrigue	❑	❑	❑
Harlequin Presents	❑	❑	❑
Harlequin Temptation	❑	❑	❑
Harlequin Blaze	❑	❑	❑
Silhouette Special Edition	❑	❑	❑
Silhouette Romance	❑	❑	❑
Silhouette Intimate Moments	❑	❑	❑
Silhouette Desire	❑	❑	❑

2. Which of the following best describes why you bought *this book?* One answer only, please.

the picture on the cover	❑	the title	❑
the author	❑	the line is one I read often	❑
part of a miniseries	❑	saw an ad in another book	❑
saw an ad in a magazine/newsletter	❑	a friend told me about it	❑
I borrowed/was given this book	❑	other: _____	❑

3. Where did you buy *this book?* One answer only, please.

at Barnes & Noble	❑	at a grocery store	❑
at Waldenbooks	❑	at a drugstore	❑
at Borders	❑	on eHarlequin.com Web site	❑
at another bookstore	❑	from another Web site	❑
at Wal-Mart	❑	Harlequin/Silhouette Reader Service/through the mail	❑
at Target	❑		
at Kmart	❑	used books from anywhere	❑
at another department store or mass merchandiser	❑	I borrowed/was given this book	❑

4. On average, how many Harlequin and Silhouette books do you buy at one time?

I buy _____ books at one time	❑
I rarely buy a book	❑

MRQ403SD-1A

5. How many times per month do you shop for any *Harlequin and/or Silhouette* books?
One answer only, please.

1 or more times a week	❏	a few times per year	❏
1 to 3 times per month	❏	less often than once a year	❏
1 to 2 times every 3 months	❏	never	❏

6. When you think of your ideal heroine, which *one* statement describes her the best?
One answer only, please.

She's a woman who is strong-willed	❏	She's a desirable woman	❏
She's a woman who is needed by others	❏	She's a powerful woman	❏
She's a woman who is taken care of	❏	She's a passionate woman	❏
She's an adventurous woman	❏	She's a sensitive woman	❏

7. The following statements describe types or genres of books that you may be
interested in reading. Pick *up to 2 types* of books that you are most interested in.

I like to read about truly romantic relationships ❏
I like to read stories that are sexy romances ❏
I like to read romantic comedies ❏
I like to read a romantic mystery/suspense ❏
I like to read about romantic adventures ❏
I like to read romance stories that involve family ❏
I like to read about a romance in times or places that I have never seen ❏
Other: _____ ❏

*The following questions help us to group your answers with those readers who are
similar to you. Your answers will remain confidential.*

8. Please record your year of birth below.
19 ____

9. What is your marital status?
single ❏   married ❏   common-law ❏   widowed ❏
divorced/separated ❏

10. Do you have children 18 years of age or younger currently living at home?
yes ❏   no ❏

11. Which of the following best describes your employment status?
employed full-time or part-time ❏   homemaker ❏   student ❏
retired ❏   unemployed ❏

12. Do you have access to the Internet from either home or work?
yes ❏   no ❏

13. Have you ever visited eHarlequin.com?
yes ❏   no ❏

14. What state do you live in?
_____

15. Are you a member of Harlequin/Silhouette Reader Service?
yes ❏   Account # _____   no ❏   MRQ403SD-1B

If you enjoyed what you just read,
then we've got an offer you can't resist!

Take 2 bestselling
love stories FREE!

Plus get a FREE surprise gift!

SOCIAL GRACES
by Dixie Browning
(Silhouette Desire #1550)

While struggling to prove his brother's
innocence in a corporate scandal, can
a rugged marine archaeologist resist his
sizzling attraction to the pampered socialite
who might be involved in the crime?

*Available December 2003
at your favorite retail outlet.*

COMING NEXT MONTH

#1549 PASSIONATELY EVER AFTER—Metsy Hingle
Dynasties: The Barones
Dot-com millionaire Steven Conti refused to let a supposed family curse
keep him from getting what he wanted: Maria Barone. The dark-haired
doe-eyed beauty that had shared his bed, refused to share his life, his home.
Now Steven would do anything to get—and keep—the woman who haunted
him still.

#1550 SOCIAL GRACES—Dixie Browning
Pampered socialites were a familiar breed to marine archaeologist
John Leo MacBride. But Valerie Bonnard, whose father's alleged crimes
had wrongly implicated his brother, was not what she appeared. Valerie
passionately believed in her father's innocence. And soon John and Valerie
were uncovering more than the truth....they were uncovering
true passions.

#1551 LONETREE RANCHERS: COLT—Kathie DeNosky
Three years before, Colt Wakefield had broken Kaylee Simpson's heart,
leaving heartache and—unknowingly—a baby growing inside her. Now,
Colt was back, demanding to get to know his daughter. Kaylee had never
been able to resist Colt, but could staying at Lonetree Ranch lead to
anything but Kaylee's seduction?

#1552 THORN'S CHALLENGE—Brenda Jackson
A charity calendar needed a photograph of the infamous
Thorn Westmoreland to increase its sales. But he would only agree
to pose for Tara Matthews in exchange for a week of her exclusive
company. If being with each other five minutes had both their hearts
racing, how would they survive a week without falling into bed?

#1553 LOCKED UP WITH A LAWMAN—Laura Wright
Texas Cattleman's Club: The Stolen Baby
Clint Andover had been given a simple mission: protect mystery woman
Jane Doe and nurse Tara Roberts from an unknown enemy. But that job
was proving anything but simple with a stubborn woman like Tara. She
challenged him at every turn...and the sparks flying between them became
flames that neither could control....

#1554 CHRISTMAS BONUS, STRINGS ATTACHED—Susan Crosby
Behind Closed Doors
Private investigator Nate Caldwell had only hired Lyndsey McCord to
pose as his temporary wife for an undercover assignment. Yet, sharing
close quarters with the green-eyed temptress had Nate forgetting their
marriage was only pretend. Falling for an employee was against company
policy...until their passion convinced Nate to change the rules!

SDCNM1103